George H. Harris

Aboriginal Occupation of the Lower Genesee Country

George H. Harris

Aboriginal Occupation of the Lower Genesee Country

ISBN/EAN: 9783337230913

Printed in Europe, USA, Canada, Australia, Japan

Cover: Foto ©Andreas Hilbeck / pixelio.de

More available books at **www.hansebooks.com**

OF THE

LOWER GENESEE COUNTRY

G[...]

1884

.

The ..... p.. the .... of the Semi-centennial History
of Rochester, N. Y., edited by Wm. F. Peck and published by D. Mason & Co.

HISTORY

OF THE

CITY OF ROCHESTER.

CHAPTER I.

ABORIGINAL OCCUPATION OF THE LOWER GENESEE COUNTRY.[1]

Antiquity of Man — Antediluvian Relics — The Ancient Beach of Lake Ontario Inhabited by Man.

THE aboriginal occupation of America is a subject of exhaustless research. Among the many divisions of this subject none present so broad a field of observation to the thoughtful investigator as the antique remains of the continent. The inquiry regarding their origin, and its direct bearing on the question of man's early history, opens the door of discussion to subjects diverse in character, comprehending nearly every line of thought and course of study. The prominence given to these antiquities has engaged the attention of men of every nationality and station in life, resulting in many ably-fought battles between earnest advocates of dissimilar views.

The interest in such remains is not alone confined to those found in America. The Old world has celebrated in prose and verse the antiquities of ancient empires and the relics of nations and tribes of primitive people to whom it is not difficult to trace an historical connection; while men of the highest scientific attainments engage in the collection and collation of evidences of the antiquity of the human race. The New world possesses no record of historic reference whereby the truth respecting her primitive peoples can be established. The fragmentary knowledge possessed by historians is derived from evidences furnished by time-worn remains, mythology and analogous reasoning, and Foster tells us, in his admirable work, *The Pre-historic Races of the United States*, that but recently a deep feeling of distrust pervaded the public mind of this

[1] The first fifteen chapters of this work were prepared by Mr. George H. Harris.

country in reference to every discovery which is supposed to carry back the origin of man to a period antecedent to the historical era; "and yet," continues the same author, "reasoning from palæontological analogies, we ought to expect to find evidences of the human occupancy of this continent, reaching back to an antiquity as remote as on the European continent."

Happily, modern thought is progressive. The rapidity with which scientific discoveries and inventions of a marvelous, though practical nature are successively brought before the public view is exerting an appreciable influence in the preparation of the human mind for a favorable reception of vital, though recently admitted, truths; "and," remarks Sir John Lubbock, "the new views in regard to the antiquity of man, though still looked upon with distrust and apprehension, will, I doubt not, in a few years be regarded with as little disquietude as are now those discoveries in astronomy and geology which at one time excited even greater opposition."[1]

"Within the present generation," says Foster, "has been opened a sphere of investigation which has enlisted an able body of observers, whose labors have thrown a flood of light upon the question relating to our common humanity. Ethnography has been raised to the rank of the noblest of sciences. However strange these new views with regard to the origin and history of our race may appear, they cannot be disregarded. We must weigh the value of observations, and press them to their legitimate conclusions." The development of those kindred sciences, geology and palæontology, united with the results of ethnological research, during the past half-century, are truly amazing in their possibilities and effect. The revelations of science are not only revolutionising the world of thought, but actually overturning the foundations of ancient history. The New world of historians is the Old world of geologists,[2] who inform us that America was "first born among the continents, and already stretched an unbroken line of land from Nova Scotia to the far West, while Europe was represented by islands rising here and there above the sea;"[3] that the Laurentian mountains in Canada, and portions of the Adirondacks in New York — the classical grounds of American geologists — are the oldest formations in the world, and along their surf-beaten coasts were developed the earliest forms of organic life. Dawson describes the *Eozoon Canadense*, or "dawn-animal," a microscopic organism of the Laurentian foundations, and suggests the possibilities of life existent in the waters of the ocean long before the appearance of land above the surface;[4] while the character of recent discoveries tends to strengthen the belief that the origin of man, even, may be assigned to

[1] Preface of *Pre-historic Times*, by Sir John Lubbock.

[2] The early rise of the American continent was asserted, for the first time, by Foster, in his report on the mineral lands of Lake Superior. The fact is too well established to require special quotation of authorities, as nearly all works on American geology, issued subsequent to 1853, affirm the statement.

[3] Agassiz, *Geological Sketches*.

[4] *The Earth and Man*, by J. W. Dawson, p. 23.

this, the most ancient of continents. Revelations of so startling a nature are the result of patient investigations pursued by learned men, who find the chronology of the Hebrew Pentateuch, which would bring everything relating to human history within the short compass of four thousand and four years antecedent to the Christian era,[1] insufficient to account for the mutations the earth has undergone,[2] and the development of man from the low stage of wildest savagery, which all evidences prove his primitive condition to have been, to the modern plane of intellectual power and refinement.

We speak of the race of men found in possession of this continent at the time of its discovery by Europeans in the fifteenth century as the Aborigines of America, and long usage has rendered the term, in the sense in which it is applied to the Indians, peculiarly fitting, though incorrect. They were natives of America, but not its original inhabitants. There are proofs of the presence here of people who lived at so early a period of time that no authoritative reference to them has ever been found in written history. We know of their existence, and occupation of the land, only through discovery of remains of a character suggestive of the term "Mound-builders," which has become their historical designation. For the history of time and events back of the red man and the Mound-builder, we must penetrate the earth itself, and, from the evidentiary material discovered, trace or reason out a parallelism with existing forms and conditions, basing our conclusions entirely upon the principle that from the beginning of time nature has worked upon the same plan, with like forces and results as at present.

Abstruse as the question of man's antiquity may appear, it is, nevertheless, pertinent to our subject — the early human occupancy of this immediate locality. We are confident that the St. Lawrence basin and the near-lying mountain districts of New York and Canada will yet furnish material aid to science in the final solution of this great problem, but, if we attempt to trace the record of man's remote occupation of our home territory by a chain of successive events, we find many of the links of connection broken or entirely wanting; still there would seem to be some grounds for the confidence expressed, in the discovery of a certain class of ancient relics that has attracted little attention in the world of science.

In a communication to the American Antiquarian society prior to 1830 the late Dr. Samuel L. Mitchell, professor of natural history, and father of geology in the state of New York, mentioned this class of antiquities as distinguished

---

[1] The Samaritan Pentateuch places the creation of the world B.C. 4700 ; the Septuagint, 5872 ; Josephus, 4658; the Talmudists, 5344; Scaliger, 3950; Petavius, 3984; Playfair, 4007. Dr. Hales places it at 5411, and enumerates over one hundred and twenty various opinions on the subject, the difference between the latest and remotest dates being no less than 3268 years. Good Bishop Usher, whose chronological table is used in the English Bible, follows the Hebrew account, and places the creation B.C. 4004.

[2] Sir William Thomson thinks the time which has elapsed from the first foundation of a solid crust on the earth to the modern period may have been from seventy to one hundred millions of years.

entirely from those which are usually ascribed to the Indians and Mound-builders, as follows :—

"In the section of country about Fredonia. New York. on the south side of Lake Erie, are discovered objects deservedly worthy of particular and inquisitive research. . . . . . This kind of antiquities present themselves on digging from thirty to fifty feet below the surface of the ground. They occur in the form of fire-brands, split wood, ashes, coals and occasionally tools and utensils, buried to those depths."

Dr. Mitchell also expressed an earnest wish that the members of the society should exert themselves with all possible diligence to ascertain and collect facts of this description for the benefit of the geologist and historian ; in the expectation that, "if collected and methodised, conclusions could be drawn of a nature that would shed light on the ancient and traditionary history of the world." Priest tells us the relics mentioned by Dr. Mitchell were found beneath the ridge which borders the east shore of Lake Erie, and refers to their origin as "antediluvian."[1] A superficial deposit, known as the "lake ridge," similar to the one on Lake Erie, extends from Sodus, New York, westward around the head of Lake Ontario into Canada, at a distance varying from three to eight miles from the present beach of the lake. Throughout its whole extent in this state this ridge is well defined, bearing all the indications of having once been the boundary of a large body of water, and of having been produced in the same manner as the elevated beaches of the ocean and larger lakes. In height it varies from a gentle swell to sharply defined elevations fifteen to twenty feet above the surface of the ground, occasionally descending toward the lake for fifty or one hundred feet in an easy slope. Its seaward side is usually covered with coarse gravel and often with large pebbles. Professor Hall, our state geologist, says :—

" If anything were wanting in the external appearance of this ridge to convince the observer of the mode of its formation, every excavation made into it proves conclusively its origin. The lowest deposit, or foundation, is a coarse sand or gravel, and upon this a regular deposit of silt. The layer of vegetable matter is evenly spread, as if deposited from water, and afterward covered with fine sand, and to this succeeds coarse sand and gravel. Fragments of wood nearly fossilised. shells, etc., are found in digging wells and cutting channels through the ridge; and there can be no doubt of its formation by the waters of Lake Ontario, which once stood at that level."[2]

The grand Indian trail from the Genesee falls to the Niagara river passed along the summit of this ridge, and for over seventy years the white man has used it as a road-bed (for one of the most extensively traveled highways in New York) between Rochester and Lewiston. The farm of David Tomlinson is situated on the Ridge road, half a mile west of the village of Gaines, Orleans county. When first occupied in 1814 the ground was covered by forest trees of large growth, many being three and four feet in diameter, and the stumps of two, specially noted as standing over a mile north of the ridge, measured,

[1] *Antiquities of America*, by Josiah Priest.
[2] *Geology of New York. Part IV.*, p. 349.

each, nearly eight feet across the top. As far as the eye could reach in either direction the ridge in this vicinity then declined toward the lake in a smooth, unbroken grade, and about one hundred and fifty feet north of its center the clear waters of a spring bubbled forth and darted away lakeward in a tiny rivulet. From the main Indian trail on the ridge a path led down to the spring, which was well known to the Indians, who often camped in the neighborhood.

In 1824 the spring-basin was cleaned out and stoned up in the form of a well. In 1853 the water failed and the well was deepened. In 1864 the well bottom was lowered to a total depth of twenty feet. About eighteen feet below the original surface the digger came upon a quantity of brush overlying an ancient fireplace, consisting of three round stones, each about one foot in diameter, placed in the form of a triangle. A mass of charcoal and ashes surrounded the stones which were burned and blackened by fire and smoke. Several sticks were found thrust between the stones, the inner ends burned and charred as left by the expiring flames. A careful inspection of these sticks by a gentleman[1] thoroughly acquainted with the nature and grain of various woods proved them to be hemlock and ash. Some were denuded of bark and had the smooth surface usually presented by water-washed wood found on any beach. Several sticks were split, and surrounding one was a depressed ring, or indentation, as though some dull instrument had been employed in an effort to weaken or break the wood. The ashes were indurated to a degree requiring the use of a pick in their removal, and rested upon a stratum of sand, which was also in a hardened condition, being taken out in large pieces that proved to be very fine grained, with a smooth surface slightly creased in places, possibly ripple marks. When first discovered the brush was closely packed over the fireplace and had every appearance of having been forced into position by the action of water. The fireplace and all the details of its narrow[2] surroundings, which were carefully noted, clearly indicated that it had been made upon a sand-beach, and was subjected to an inundation that washed the mass of brush, possibly gathered for fuel, over the stones and ashes, which were afterward covered many feet deep by successive strata of the same gravelly soil of which the ridge is composed, and was thus preserved for ages unknown.

In a survey of the grounds and after thorough consideration of the circumstances the writer became assured of the following conclusions: The fireplace was constructed by persons having the use of rude implements and possessed of some knowledge of cookery, at a period just previous to the formation of the ridge. In its formation this ridge was extended along the base of an ele-

[1] John Nutt, of Rochester, to whose excellent knowledge of the early history of this locality the writer is indebted for many facts.

[2] In 1880 these facts, as presented, were brought to the notice of Lewis H. Morgan, of Rochester, who assured the writer that the discovery was the most interesting and valuable one within his knowledge, respecting the ridge, and he earnestly advised its publication.

vation connected with the mountain-ridge, and constituted a solid dam, from one hundred to one hundred and fifty feet wide, across the mouth of a little valley and inward curvature of the hillside. The accumulation of water, shed by the surrounding slopes, originally transformed the basins thus created into ponds, and subsequently, when drained, converted them into marshes. The valley waters, aided by the current of an inflowing stream, forced a channel through the ridge, but the waters of the small pond were gradually released by soaking through the mud bottom and following the course of a vein underneath the ridge to its northern side, where they rose to the surface in the form of a spring. The failure of the spring was caused by the clearing and cultivation of its marsh source. It is evident that the spring came into operation long after the ridge was formed, and the rise of the water directly above the fireplace was incidental, there being no connection whatever between the two events.

If these conclusions are justified by the conditions related, it would appear that man was a habitant of the south shore of Lake Ontario before the ridge existed, and, if the age of the ridge can be even approximately determined, some idea can be had of the length of time he has occupied our home territory. The results of a special study regarding the peculiar topographical features of Western New York lead to the conclusion that the ridge is of very ancient origin — in fact, that it antedates the present rock-cut channel of the Genesee — and, though our range of inquiry is necessarily limited, a brief exposition of reasons influencing this conclusion may prove of interest.

CHAPTER II.

Surface Geology — The Great Sea — Origin of the Genesee River — Great Age of the Lake Ridge — Man's Antiquity in the Genesee Country.

IN every direction about Rochester we behold the effects of aqueous action. The hills, domes and pillars of sand and gravel, the rolling plains and alluvial ridges, the great valleys and deep channels of watercourses, the polished rocks of limestone beneath the soil, and huge boulders scattered over the surface, all combine in an appeal to our reason, arouse an interest and create a desire to learn the primary cause of these singular forms of nature. The science of geology teaches that the earth first appeared above the waters of the ocean in the form of azoic rock, and those grand scientists, Agassiz and Dana, tell us that certain portions of the territory of the Empire state were among the very first kissed by the warm sunlight of heaven.

Passing over the changes occurring during many succeeding geological ages, we reach a period when the rising continent had divided the waters of the ocean by the elevation of mountain barriers, and converted all this part of America into an inland sea. The physical contour of much of the state of New York is directly due to the active agency of the waters of this sea, which left its impress upon so large an area of our natural surroundings; and its history, as revealed by geological developments, has a local application which may worthily excite an interest not usual in matters of this character. Even the noble river, quietly carrying its daily tribute of mountain waters from the Alleghanies through the heart of Rochester to Lake Ontario, has its place in the history of the great sea, and it is a curious fact that the results of scientific research show the history of the Genesee as differing from that of other rivers in the processes of its formation. The tinge of romance, lending attractiveness to all narrations of man's early acquaintance with the Genesee, deepens to a flush in the recital of the ancient river's history. The spring gushing from a hill-side, its sparkling waters finding their way to some natural depression, forms a purling brook, by small degrees and successive additions enlarging to the size of a creek, increasing in volume and magnitude to the full development of a river flowing in silent majesty, with great sweeps and curves, along its well-defined channel, crushing with irresistible force through some rock-bound mountain gorge, plunging with mighty thunderings over a great precipice into the deep basin below, and thence passing onward to lose their identity forever in the commingled floods of lake and ocean — such is the natural history of rivers.

No record like this bears the Genesee. The growth of its formation was one of recession. Not at the bubbling fountain of distant plain or hill-slope began the inceptive movement of its birth, but near its very entrance into the great fresh water sea of its deposit. Springing into life with the full force born of bursting lake barriers, its first current must have been a mighty stream of great width and power, capable of rending asunder the rock foundations of the earth; and the course now pursued from its modern headwater sources on the mountain plains of Pennsylvania is the result of a decreasing volume, narrowing its bounds from the broad expanse of its mother-lakes to the contracted space of the latest channel in the valley bottom. This, and many other facts of special interest, we learn in the history of the great sea whose boundaries, at the period of its first separation from the ocean, are not clearly defined; but an idea of their general course at a later date, when the configuration of the earth was nearly complete, can be formed by a brief study of the topography of North America, which discloses an immense basin, bounded on the north by the range of mountains extending through Canada to the far West; on the east by the New England range, extending southwesterly by the Highlands of New York and the Alleghanies of Pennsylvania, thence west and south toward the Mississippi river.

The elevation of the interior of the continent produced its natural effect in a subsidence of the sea-waters into the depressions of the earth then existing, their divisions into lesser seas, and in time by successive drainage at outlets of different elevation, the formation of lakes. The immense basin of the St. Lawrence, which extends from the gulf of St. Lawrence to the headwaters of the Mississippi — a distance of two thousand miles — formed the first reservoir. This, in time, was divided by natural barriers into three sub-basins. The first of these has an area of about 90,000 square miles, more than one-fourth of which is occupied by the waters of Lake Superior. The next, or middle, basin has an area of at least 160,000 square miles and contains Lakes Huron, Michigan and Erie in its lowest depressions. The surface of the lower basin has an area of about 260,000 square miles and is covered in part by the waters of Lake Ontario and the St. Lawrence river. The upper basin probably had its outlet into the middle basin, which, previous to the destruction of the original coast-ridge at the northeastern end of Lake Erie and consequent birth of Niagara river, had its drainage to the south through the valleys of the Des Plains, Kankakee, Illinois and Mississippi rivers, into the gulf of Mexico.[1]

The period in which the actual division of the middle and lower basins took place cannot be fixed, but the occurrence marked an era from which our interest in the subsiding waters of the great sea is confined to the lower, or Ontario, basin. About the time of this separation the Mount Hope and Pinnacle range of hills, on the southern boundary line of the city, formed a barrier at the north end of the Genesee valley, and, dividing the waters, produced a great shallow lake covering all the valley between Rochester and Dansville. The waters of the sea, now Lake Ontario, continued their retirement to the north, and coast lines formed during the period of recession can be traced at many points on the slopes of the Ontario basin where the waves left their mark on cliff and hillside, or washed up great alluvial ridges in open plains. At least a dozen such ridges can be found at different places in New York, and two at Rochester, the lake ridge being the most distinct. It is probable that a barrier across the St. Lawrence then restrained the lake waters, which escaped through the valley of the Mohawk at Little Falls into the Hudson. The lowest part of the old channel through the rocky gorge at Little Falls is 428 feet above the ocean, and the ridge in Rochester is about 441 feet.[2]   It is supposed

---

[1] *Niagara Falls and Other Famous Cataracts*, by George W. Holley. This book contains a very interesting history of the middle basin and the probable origin of the Niagara river and falls.

[2] Through the kindness of R. J. Smith, A. J. Grant and E. B. Whitmore, civil engineers, the elevation of various points between the upper Genesee fall and Lake Ontario, which has never been published before, has been obtained. The ridge at the intersection of the Charlotte boulevard west of Hanford's Landing, is 193.91 feet above Lake Ontario. At the crossing of the Ontario Belt railroad, about 1,000 feet east of the river, the ridge is 182.45 feet above the lake. The latter, according to the recent (1878) geodetic survey, is 247.25 feet above the ocean. An influx of water rising 247.25 feet above mean tide at New York would place the ocean on a level with Lake Ontario; 441 feet, with the ridge, and connect the lake with the Hudson river through the Mohawk valley at Little Falls; 508 feet, with

that the waters had retired beyond the level of the ridge, and from some unknown cause — possibly the breaking down of the natural obstruction at the northeastern extremity of Lake Erie, and discharge of its waters into Lake Ontario — again rose several feet, the ridge being formed under the water while the surface was but a few feet above. The breaking away, or removal, of the St. Lawrence barrier reduced the lake to its present level.

Following this event, the Genesee valley lake burst through the hills east of the Pinnacle, formed a great river, now the Genesee, and excavated the bay of Irondequoit.[1] In time this channel became obstructed and the waters cut a new outlet through the hill west of the present channel at the Rapids in South Rochester, pursuing a direct northern course to the present Genesee falls in the heart of the city. This passage becoming obstructed just north of the Rapids, the river was directed east toward Mount Hope and thence northward through its modern channel. The production of the Genesee river gorge through Rochester to Lake Ontario is mainly the result of erosion, having been effected by running water aided by frost, and it is evident that this work has been accomplished since Lake Ontario retired from the ridge. If this theory is correct — and it is affirmed by scientists[2] — the lake ridge antedates the Genesee river and Irondequoit bay, and the fireplace discovered on the old beach beneath the ridge at Gaines was constructed by men who occupied our home territory at a period so remote that it is not possible to fix its limit. It may be stated, however, that, from deductions covering the age of supposed contemporaneous events, it has been crudely estimated as exceeding fourteen thousand years.

the Erie canal aqueduct in Rochester, and submerge half the city; 573.58 feet with Lake Erie; 588 feet, with Lake Michigan; 600 feet would carry the waters over the dividing plateau between Chicago and the Mississippi valley and re-establish the great interior sea, with the ocean flowing from Labrador to the gulf of Mexico. The sea would be 353 feet above the present level of Lake Ontario, and Rochester submerged but ninety-two feet at the aqueduct. The tops of many buildings in the city would remain above the surface. Pinnacle hill, in the shape of a conical island, would rise seventy-one feet above the water, and Mount Hope and the intervening range form a cluster of knolls and line of shallow bars.

[1] Professor James Hall, *Geological Survey of the Fourth District*.

[2] See *Illustrations of Surface Geology* and *Erosions of the Earth's Surface*, by Edward Hitchcock, LL.D.; *Smithsonian Contributions to Knowledge, Vol. IX.; Geology of New York*, by James Hall, and other standard works.

CHAPTER III.

Ancient Races — The Mound-builders — The White Woman of the Genesee — Traditions of the Red Men — Presence of a Pre-historic People in the Genesee Valley, and about Irondequoit Bay — The Ridge Mounds and Relics — Ancient Landings on the Genesee — A Race of Large Men.

THAT a race, or races, of men preceded the Indians in the occupation of this country is too well understood to require special iteration. We may never learn the origin of those ancient people, or gather more than scattering lines of their history, but tangible, imperishable proofs of their former presence on a large area of the American continent still remain in the form of earthworks which extend from New York westwardly along the southern shore of Lake Erie, and through Michigan and the intermediate states and territories to the Pacific. They have been found on the shores of Lake Pepin, and on the Missouri river over one thousand miles above its junction with the Mississippi, and extend down the valley of the latter to the gulf of Mexico. They line the shores of the gulf from Texas to Florida, continue in diminished numbers into South Carolina,[1] and stand as eternal sentinels on the Rio Grande del Norte.

The age in which the Mound-builder lived and flourished is at present undetermined; it may yet be decided as contemporaneous with that of ancient nations known to civilised man, or at some definite period beyond the present measurements of written history. The theory generally accepted places the Mound-builders in possession of this country at the advent of the Indians, who dispossessed and nearly exterminated the original owners of the soil. The survivors of the conquered people fled down the Mississippi valley, and are supposed to have mingled with tribes of red men that followed them. In his new work, the *Iroquois Book of Rites*, page 11, Mr. Hale says he has found traces in the Cherokee tongue of a foreign language, which he supposes to have been derived from the Mound-builders of the Ohio valley, whom he identifies as the Allegewi, or Tallegewi. According to the legends of the Iroquois and Algonkins, those two races of red men united in a war against, and overpowered, the Allegewi, who, says Mr. Hale, "left their name to the Alleghany river and mountains, and whose vast earthworks are still, after half a century of study, the perplexity of archæologists."

While these monuments are not generally supposed to exist beyond the tributary sources of the Alleghany, in Western New York, there would appear to be reasonable grounds for a belief that the Mound-builders, or other ancient people, extended their settlements into the interior of the state, and dwelt here in considerable numbers. During the old French war, in 1755, a party of French and Indians attacked a frontier settlement in Pennsylvania, murdered a number of the inhabitants and carried away several women and

---

[1] *Antiquities of New York and the West*, by E. G. Squier, p. 294.

children as captives. Among the latter was a little girl, who was adopted by a Seneca family, grew to womanhood, became the wife of two Indian warriors, reared several children, and for nearly eighty years held no family or social relationship other than that of her Indian associates, to whom she was known as Deh-he-wa-mis. Her name was Mary Jemison, but for over a century the people of her own race have designated her "the white woman of the Genesee," the greater part of her life being spent in the vicinity of the Genesee river. At the great council held at Big Tree (Geneseo) in 1797 her Indian friends stipulated that Mrs. Jemison should receive a tract of land located on the Genesee between Mount Morris and Portage. The river passes through this land in a deep, narrow valley, and the fertile land on the valley bottom, where the white woman made her home, is known as Gardeau flats. In Seaver's *Life of Mary Jemison*, page 134, we find the following statements, received from her own lips :—

"About three hundred acres of my land when I first saw it were open flats lying on the Genesee river, which it is supposed were cleared by a race of inhabitants who preceded the first Indian settlements in this part of the country. The Indians are confident that many parts of this country were settled, and for a number of years occupied, by a people of whom their fathers never had any traditions, as they never had seen them. Whence these people originated, and whither they went, I have never heard one of the oldest and wisest Indians pretend to guess. When I first came to Genishau, the bank of Fall brook had just slid off, exposing a large number of human bones, which the Indians said were buried there long before their fathers ever saw the place, and they did not know what kind of people they were. It, however, was, and is, believed by our people that they were not Indians. . . . . The tradition of the Seneca Indians in regard to their origin is that they broke out of the earth from a large mountain at the head of Canandaigua lake, and that mountain they still venerate as the place of their birth. Thence they derive their name 'Ge-nun-da-wah,' or 'Great Hill People.' The Senecas have a tradition that previous to, and for some time after, their origin at Genundawah, the country, especially about the lakes, was thickly inhabited by a race of civil, enterprising and industrious people who were totally destroyed by the great serpent that afterward surrounded the great hill fort, with the assistance of others of the same species, and that they (the Senecas) went into possession of the improvements left."

Near the top of a high ridge of sand hills, in the town of Pittsford, south of the Irondequoit valley, and about one mile east of Allen's creek, stands a great heap of limestone boulders, evidently of drift origin. They are the only stone of that character in that vicinity, measure from two to three feet in diameter, and are heaped one upon the other in a space about twelve feet square. They occupied the same place and position sixty or seventy years ago, and old residents say the heap existed in the same form when the ground was cleared. Indians who passed that way in early days regarded the stones with superstitious awe, stating, when questioned, that a people who lived there before the Indians brought the stones to the hilltop.

"On the shore of Lake Ontario, on a high bluff near Irondequoit bay, in 1796," says Oliver Culver, "the bank caved off and untombed a great quantity of human bones, of a large size. The arm and leg bones, upon comparison, were much larger than those of our own race."[1] The bluff mentioned by Mr. Culver was the seaward side of an elevated spot that might properly be termed a natural mound. It was one of the outlying range of sand hills or knolls, then existent along the shore of the lake in that locality, and long years ago succumbed to the never-ceasing encroachment of the lake waters. Its location was immediately west of the angle formed by the present west line of Irondequoit bay and Lake Ontario; as late as 1830 human bones of an unusually large size were occasionally seen projecting from the face of the bluff, or lying on the beach where the undermined soil had fallen. The tribe of Seneca Indians living in Irondequoit in 1796 could give no information concerning these bones, stating their belief that they were the remains of a people who dwelt about the bay before the Indians came there.

The town of Irondequoit north of the ridge was known as the "pine barrens" to the early settlers who cleared it of a heavy growth of pine trees, many of which stood upon the top of the bluff, and over the ancient cemetery, sixty years ago. The French historians of DeNonville's invasion of the Indian towns in this vicinity, in 1687, describe the country east of Irondequoit bay at that date, as covered with tall woods sufficiently open to allow the army to march in three columns. These facts clearly show that if the land about Irondequoit bay was once cleared and cultivated, as some infer, it was at quite an early period, and by people known only through tradition to the latter-day Indians.

During his investigation of the aboriginal monuments of New York, in 1848, Mr. Squier visited several located within the bounds of Monroe county, and spent considerable time in fruitless search for an ancient inclosure and mounds, which he had been informed existed at an early date in Irondequoit near the Genesee river. In his valuable work,[2] published soon after, he expressed a hope that the discovery of these monuments might reward the labors of a future explorer. Long and patient searches for the works mentioned by Mr Squier were made some years ago without success, and in 1879 the circumstance was casually alluded to in the presence of the writer's aged mother, who, at once, located the mounds and gave an excellent description of their primitive appearance.

In its course from the upper falls in Rochester. to Lake Ontario the Genesee river flows in a deep, valley-like channel formed by ages of attrition. From the lower falls to within three-fourths of a mile of the lake, the east bank rises in a nearly perpendicular wall, varying from one hundred to two hun-

---

[1] *Phelps and Gorham Purchase*, p. 428.
[2] *Antiquities of New York*, p. 58.

dred and fifty feet in height,[1] broken at intervals by the deeply worn outlets of creeks and brooklets. At the northern limit of the city, half a mile below the lower falls, a great break occurs in the bluff, which curves inward, forming a crude semi-circle. Immense quantities of detritus have accumulated at the bottom, and slope up the face of the precipice, affording room for a narrow flat along the water, and opportunity for man to construct a roadway which winds in a serpentine course up the steep bank to the level land above. This is the only place on the east side of the river between the falls and lake where easy communication can be effected between the general surface of the land and the river bed. It constitutes a natural landing-place, and is practically the head of navigation from Lake Ontario. The western end of the lake ridge, at its severance by the river, rests upon the top of the cliff directly above the landing. At the southern base of the ridge are the ice ponds of Messrs. Emerson and Brewer, fed by the waters of springs which rise a short distance east.

The locality was formerly a grand camping-ground of the Indians, the last one of that fated race who set up his wigwam on the ridge, in 1845, commemorating the event by the murder of his squaw. It was undoubtedly one of the most noted points between Lake Erie and the Hudson river, and as well known to the people who preceded the Indians as to the latter. From its commanding situation overlooking the river in both directions, its nearness to the landing and trails which converged there, the adaptability of the soil for easy handling by the rude implements of the natives, and many other natural advantages of the neighborhood, it was the place preferable above all others upon which to erect burial mounds, and two of these, evidently of artificial origin, existed there when the first settlers made their homes near the lower falls. These mounds were about four feet high and twenty or twenty-five feet across the base. They occupied the most elevated portion of the ridge, and were situated from seventy-five to one hundred feet east of the edge of the bluff, and about the same distance north of and parallel with the present line of Brewer's pond.

At the time Mr. Squier made his search the ground was, or had been, under cultivation and the mounds reduced to nearly the level of the natural ridge. When examined in 1879 no satisfactory conclusion could be reached regarding their manner of construction, though it was plainly observable in places that

---

[1] To the scientist the immediate vicinity of Rochester must ever present attractions unsurpassed by those of other localities. Especially is this true in the splendid facilities afforded the geologist to minutely examine the works of nature, and pursue his favorite study within her very laboratory, the deep, rock-cut channel of the Genesee river. This fact was well understood at an early day, and sketches illustrating the escarpment of the lower Genesee adorn many standard works on geology. *Dana's Manual*, page 90, illustrates a section, four hundred feet in height, of the strata as exhibited along the Genesee, at the lower falls. This section has a world-wide fame as fairly illustrating the structure and arrangement of stratified rocks in their chronological order; and no series of natural rocks could be finer, as the transition from one stratum to another is quite abrupt, and, moreover, each may be traced for a long distance through the adjoining country.

sand, intermixed with clay, covered the original surface of the ground to the depth of a foot. Fragments of chipped flint, arrow-heads and stone knives were picked up in considerable number near the mounds, and, on digging one or two feet into the ground, bits of charcoal, several rude points and a broken spear head of stone were unearthed.

In 1880 a sand bank was opened in the side of the ridge, and that part covered by the mounds has since been entirely removed. During the course of excavation a laborer came upon human remains. Parts of eight skeletons were exhumed, each surrounded by fine black soil. These were concealed and all evidence of the find destroyed; but the discovery of a bone of unusual size, together with a curious pipe, was brought to the attention of Mr. Brewer. The laborer could remember few details of the position in which the remains were found, and the opportunity for careful investigation was lost.

The Mound-builders were inveterate smokers, and great numbers of pipes have been found in their mounds. The skill of the makers seems to have been exhausted in their construction, and no specimens of Indian art can equal those of the lost race. Many pipes of a shape similar to those discovered in the mounds of the Ohio and Mississippi valleys have been found in various parts of the country. Figure 1 is a greatly reduced representation of an article of

FIG. 1.

stone, evidently intended for a pipe, but unfinished, found near Mount Morris, in the Genesee valley, and sent to the New York state cabinet at Albany by Mr. Squier, who says: "It is composed of steatite or 'soap-stone,' and in shape corresponds generally with the pipes of stone found in the mounds of the Mississippi valley. One or two pipes of stone of very nearly the same shape have been found in the same vicinity, but in point of symmetry or finish they are in no way comparable to those of the mounds."[1] The pipe taken from the ridge mound in Rochester is of the distinctively characteristic, or primitive form[2] peculiar to the Mound-builders, and is represented in figure 2. It is, or was originally, five and one-half inches long, one and three-fourths wide, and one inch and seven-eighths from bottom of base to top of bowl. The lines are slightly irregular, but very perfect for a hand-made article. The material is steatite, very close grain and quite brittle. In color it is a deep,

[1] *Antiquities of New York*, p. 118.
[2] *Ancient Monuments of the Mississippi Valley*, p. 227.

rich brown, with blending patches of lighter shade, and every particle of the surface is so beautifully polished that it might easily be mistaken for marble. It was the only article of any description found with the human remains, though other relics may have been unnoticed. Close questioning elicited the fact that

FIG. 2.

nearly all the graves were near the south slope of the ridge, and from two to two and a half feet below the original surface, while the large bone, a humerus, was nearer the surface and perhaps more directly beneath the center of the west mound; from which it may be inferred, though not definitely proven, that the mound was built over that particular body with which the pipe was buried, and the other bodies interred in the side of the mound at a subsequent period. The condition of the remains would seem to favor this view, the humerus being the only remaining part of the body to which it belonged, while several portions of skeletons from the other graves were, though very much decayed, quite firm in comparison; one skull (figure 3) being preserved entire. Mr.

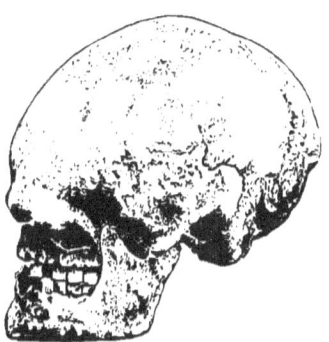

FIG. 3.

Brewer presented this skull and pipe to Professor S. A. Lattimore of the University of Rochester, to whom we are indebted for their use.

In March, 1882, a human skeleton of large proportions was unearthed near the former location of the east mound. The laborers, astonished at the great size of the bones, engaged in a discussion as to whether it was or was not the remains of a human being, and, with true Hibernian method, *broke the skeleton into fragments to prove the case.*

As previously stated, the only landing on the east side of the lower Genesee is at the base of the bluff upon which the ridge mounds were situated, and is now known as Brewer's landing. In their journey from the lower to the upper Genesee, the Indians usually made a portage around the falls of Rochester, carrying their canoes from this landing to near the mouth of Red creek, above the rapids in South Rochester, where the light crafts were again launched upon the river and found a clear passage up the unobstructed channel to Mount Morris. That was the established route one hundred years ago, but good and valid reasons induce a belief that the more ancient landing was at Hanford's, on the west bank of the Genesee, about one-fourth of a mile below, or north of Brewer's landing; and that the two places were connecting points in a general highway extending east and west along the ridge. Evidence is not wanting to prove that another grand road once extended westward from Hanford's landing, with diverging branches running to distant points. This road was not in use some miles west of the river one hundred years ago, and that portion of it has probably been abandoned for two or three centuries; but, possessing a general knowledge of Indian methods of trailing, the topography of the country, and the probable objective points, the writer is slowly tracing the course of this older highway from the Genesee at Rochester to the Alleghany and Ohio rivers and Lake Erie.

Discoveries have been made, at various places along this supposed route, of mounds and burial grounds containing human skeletons considerably larger than men of the present day, copper ornaments, etc., and one or two instances will be given. In excavating for sand on the farm of Samuel Truesdale, in the town of Greece, in 1878, several skeletons were disinterred, one from its immense size attracting particular attention. Nearly the entire frame was secured and removed to a level spot between two trees, where Warren Truesdale placed each bone in its natural position. The skeleton thus reformed measured over eight feet in length. A piece of mica and a rude arrow point were found in the grave above the bones, which were about three feet below the general surface, and entirely separate from the other skeletons. A small mound, perhaps a foot in height, marked the spot.

Half a mile west of Mr. Truesdale's farm the Erie canal turns abruptly to the west along the brow of the mountain-ridge, and constitutes the northern boundary of George H. Lee's farm. The ridge at this place rises in a gentle swell above the surrounding surface, and, at its highest part, is from sixteen to twenty feet above the canal bottom. The ground was cleared in 1818, by David Oviatt, of a dense forest of beech and maple, many of the trees being full thirty inches in diameter. Not the slightest trace of former settlement or human occupation of the ground existed. In 1820 or 1822 the Erie canal was constructed through the northern slope of this ridge. During the work some twenty skeletons were exhumed from the ground directly beneath the stumps of the forest trees. The soil is composed of from six to twelve inches of black mould overlying a bed of clay, very compact when *in situ*, but loose-grained and easily crumbled when exposed to the atmosphere. So tenacious is the character of this clay bed, excluding to a great degree both air and water, that all larger bones of the skeletons were preserved in perfect form, from skull to instep inclusive; some of them being carefully uncovered and the bones laid in their natural order on the ground, measured from seven feet upward.[1] No article of any description was found in the graves. In 1879 a beautiful cling-stone ax was plowed up in a field near the ancient burial ground. It is very hard, gives forth a clear metallic sound when struck, and the edge is as finely beveled as a steel ax of modern make. It is a splendid specimen of polished stone workmanship, ten and a half inches long, two and a half wide and one and a half inches thick.

Dependent as certain of these statements are upon the results of future research for a correct understanding of their relative worth and bearing, the advance of specific conclusions regarding the subject in question might appear unwise; but, while the discovery of lately existing monuments and traces of a people superior to the red men in physical structure, the mythology of the latter and other evidence of a similar nature serve to strengthen a personal belief in the pre-Indian occupation of our home territory, the facts presented, and many matters not here shown, are but minor paragraphs of a volume of cumulative evidence that might be compiled. Such facts have exercised an influence upon reflective minds leading to firm conviction, and able writers have repeatedly affirmed the conclusion. Governor De Witt Clinton, an early historian of the locality of Rochester, was particularly impressed with this idea, and Orsamus Turner, author of the *History of the Holland Purchase*, reiterates it in numerous passages of his works. He says: —

"Our advent here is but one of the changes of time. We are consulting dumb signs, inanimate and unintelligible witnesses, gleaning but unsatisfactory knowledge of races that have preceded us. . . . . We are surrounded by evidences that a race preceded them (the red men), further advanced in arts, and far more numerous. The uprooted trees of the forest, that are the growth of centuries, expose their mouldering remains, uncovered mounds reveal masses of their skeletons. . . . . In our valleys, upon our hillsides, the plow and the spade discover their rude implements, adapted to war, the chase and domestic use. All these are dumb, yet eloquent chronicles of bygone ages. . . . . We are prone to speak of ourselves as inhabitants of a New world, and yet we are confronted with these evidences of antiquity. We clear away the forests and speak familiarly of subduing a virgin soil; yet our plows upturn the skulls of those whose history is lost."

[1] *Junior Pioneer Historical Collections*, by Jarvis M. Hatch, p. 29. This statement was confirmed by the late Wilson D. Oviatt, Daniel E. Harris and others.

CHAPTER IV.

The Red Men — Their Traditional Origin and Occupation of New York — Dispersion of the Tribes — League of the Iroquois — Vale of the Senecas — Ancient Nations of the Genesee Country.

PUZZLING as the remains of the Mound-builders prove to the archæologist, the early history of their Indian successors is no less a problem to the historian. Nearly four centuries have elapsed since Europeans came into personal intercourse with the latter, and half a million of the race still exist upon American soil, yet their origin is buried in the depths of a gloom so profound that no man has ever traced it to its source.

The length of time our Indian predecessors have occupied this continent has never been ascertained, though it is unquestionably a fact that they were not indigenous. The weight of evidence thus far favors the theory of Asiatic descent, but in "the absence of written, pictorial, or sculptural history it is impossible to trace clearly the connection between wandering savages and their remote ancestry."[1] Centuries of nomadic and climatic changes have effectually obliterated direct proof of such connections; and Indian mythology asserts the origin of many tribes as local to their habitation.

The Senecas ascribe their origin to a great hill at the head of Canandaigua lake, but Morgan explains that "by this legendary invention they designed to convey an impression of the remoteness of the period of their first occupation of New York,"[2] and presents other traditionary evidences showing the lower St. Lawrence[3] to have been the earliest known abode of the original families from which the Six Nations were descended. These ancient people were of the Huron-Iroquois stock. They were expelled from the lower St. Lawrence by the Algonkins, to whom they had been subject, and migrated westward up that river. Entering Lake Ontario they coasted the south shore in search of a suitable place to locate. Historical accounts of this migration vary. Macauley states that the Iroquois then consisted of only two tribes, the Mohawks and Senecas, that they entered the Oswego and Genesee rivers, conquered the Mohawk and Genesee countries first, and the intermediate space subsequently.[4] President Dwight believed the original settlements of the Six Nations in New York to have been identical with those in which they were found by Europeans, while Colden and Smith thought the Iroquois originated and remained upon the grounds of their latter-time occupation. Morgan says that at the migration from the St. Lawrence the Iroquois entered the central parts of New York through the channel of the Oswego river. Their first settlements

---

[1] *How the World was Peopled*, by Edward Fontaine.

[2] *League of the Iroquois*, p. 7.

[3] *Ibid.*, p. 5; see also Colden, *History of the Five Nations*, p. 23; Cusic. *Ancient History of the Six Nations*, p. 16.

[4] Macauley's *History of New York*, vol. 2, p. 184.

were located upon the Seneca river, where for a time they dwelt together. At
a subsequent day they divided into bands, and spread to found new villages. [1]
In his interesting work, *Legends, Customs and Social Life of the Seneca
Indians*, Rev. Mr. Sanborn gives a legend still preserved in that nation, which
makes all Indians the descendants of one family originally located where now
are New York and Brooklyn. It describes the migrations and final location of
tribes, in nearly the same manner as Cusic's account. The latter's quaint
history appears to be the version from which several others were derived. In
the *Iroquois Book of Rites*, Mr. Hale follows Cusic, who supposes a body of
Iroquois concealed in a mountain near the Oswego falls. Upon their libera-
tion by the "Holder of the Heavens," they went around a mountain and
followed the Mohawk and Hudson rivers to the ocean. Some of the people
continued southward, but the main company, under the guidance of the
Holder of the Heavens, returned up the Hudson to the Mohawk river.
Along this stream and the upper waters of the Hudson the first families made
their abode. Their language was soon altered and they were named Te-haw-
re-ho-geh—that is, "a speech divided"— now Mohawk.[2] The other families
journeyed westward from the Mohawks, and, halting at various places, took
up separate abodes. The Oneidas, near a creek, were termed Ne-haw-re-
tah-go, or Big Tree people; the Onondagas, on a mountain, were known
as the Seuh-now-kah-tah, "carrying their name;" the Cayugas, near a
long lake, were named Sho-nea-na-we-to-wah, "a great pipe;" the Senecas,
near a high mountain south of Canandaigua lake, received the name Te-how-
nea-nyo-hent, "possessing a door."

The sixth family continued their journey toward the setting sun and
touched the bank of the great lake Kau-ha-gwa-rah-ka ("a cap"), now Lake
Erie. Turning southward they came to a great river, which Cusic designates
the Mississippi, but which Hale shows to have been the Ohio; the people discovered a grape vine lying across the river and attempted to pass over the
water on this rude bridge, which broke and left them divided. Those who
were upon the further side of the river continued their way, and after long

---

[1] *League of the Iroquois*, p. 6.

[2] Hale says the Huron speech became the Iroquois tongue, in the form in which it is spoken by the
Mohawks. In Iroquois tradition, and in the constitution of their league, the Mohawk nation ranks as
the eldest brother of the family. A comparison of the dialects proves the tradition to be well founded.
The Mohawk language approaches the nearest to the Huron, and is undoubtedly the source from
which all other Iroquois dialects are derived. Mr. Hale refers to the Mohawks as the Caniengas. The
latter designation is said to be derived from that of one of their ancient towns. This name is Kani-
enke, "at the flint." Kamien, in their language, signifies flint, and the final syllable is the same
locative particle which we find in Onontake, "at the mountain." In pronunciation and spelling, this,
like other Indian words, is much varied, both by the natives themselves and by their white neighbors,
becoming Kanieke, Kanyenke, Canyengeh and Canienga. (The latter form, which accords with the
sister names of Onondaga and Cayuga, is adopted by the author in his *Book of Rites*, but it is not
probable that the word will ever displace the familiar historical designation—Mohawk).

wandering settled near the mouth of the Neuse river. They were named Kau-to-nah, and are now known as Tuscaroras.[1]

The speech of all the nations thus formed was altered, but not to an extent preventing them from an understanding of one another's language. The people left upon the near side of the river were dispersed, and each family sought residences according to their convenience.[2] The various accounts of this dispersion are meager, but it is believed that all nations and tribes of red men who occupied the country between Canandaigua lake and Lake Erie, the Alleghany mountains and Lake Ontario, were offshoots of the Senecas; that the dispersed families in time grew into tribal communities and were known by various names. Those who settled about the mountains to the south were called Andastes, Canestogas, etc. Those who dwelt along the shore of the lake were known as the Eries, and northeast of them were the Attiwandaronks. Philologists assert that the languages of all these people, so far as can be ascertained, differed but little from the Seneca tongue; but it is certain that long anterior to the white man's intrusion on the soil of Western New York they had become nations distinct from the Seneca. Cusic and Sanborn agree in the statement that the famous league of the Five Nations was formed at a period not long subsequent to the dispersion, but in the loose chronology of the Indians' verbal history no definite idea of dates can be obtained. It is only by comparison with some contemporary event recorded in the annals of civilisation, that the time of the occurrence can be fixed. Morgan places the origin of the league in 1459,[3] and this date is in accordance with deductions of later historians.

The founder of the league was an Onondaga chieftain named Hiawatha, who succeeded in uniting the Mohawks, Oneidas, Onondagas, Cayugas and Senecas in one great family, whose bond of common interest was strengthened by ties of blood. To the English they were known as the Five Nations. By the French they were called Iroquois, and that name was applied to all the members of the league. The native name of the confederacy is given differently by historians, but all agree upon its signification. According to Cusic it was Ggo-nea-seah-neh. Macauley and Hale, both of whom derived their information directly from the Mohawks, render it respectively Aganuschioni and Kanonsionni. Morgan, whose knowledge of the Six Nations was acquired from the Senecas, states that after the formation of the league, the Iroquois called themselves the Ho-de-no-sau-nee, which signifies "the people of the long house." It grew out of the circumstance that they likened their confed-

[1] In the Seneca dialect the name of the Tuscaroras was Dus-ga-o-weh, "the shirt-wearing people;" the Cayugas were Gue-u-gweh-o-no, "the people at the mucky land;" the Onondagas were Onun-da-ga-o-no, "the people on the hills;" the Oneidas were O-na-yote-ha, "the granite people;" the Mohawks, Ga-ne-a-ga-o-no; the Senecas, Nun-da-wa-o-no.—Morgan, pp. 51 and 52.

[2] Cusic's *Ancient History of the Six Nations.*

[3] *Systems of Consanguinity and Affinity of the Human Family*, p. 151.

cracy to a long house, having partitions and separate fires, after their ancient
method of building houses, within which the several nations were sheltered
under one roof.[1] The eastern door was on the Hudson river, the western door
at the Genesee. The confederation was simply for common defense, and each
nation or canton was a sovereign republic, composed of clans, governed by its
own chiefs and sachems. No enterprise of importance was ever undertaken,
either by the league, or by individual nations, without first considering the
matter in council. The great councils of the league were held at Onondaga,
but each nation and tribe had a particular location for its council fire, which
was always lighted before deliberations began. The primeval council fire of
the Senecas was at Genundawah, near the head of Canandaigua lake, and in
the light of its steady flame were formed the first war parties of the nation
From Genundawah the Senecas went forth upon their first expeditions against
tribes to the west, and there the victorious warriors were welcomed home from
battle with all the pomp of barbaric fashion.

Before the Senecas crossed the Genesee in conquest, several nations of red
men occupied the land to the west. Those who owned the country bordering
the lower Genesee were called Kak-kwas by the Senecas, and were known to
the French as the Attiwandaronk, or Neutral Nation. Brebeuf, the Jesuit, says
the name Attiwandaronk was applied to them by the Hurons, and signifies
"people of a language a little different." The French termed them Neutral,
from the fact that they took no part in the war between the Hurons, Algonkins
and Iroquois. Members of those antagonistic nations met upon neutral ground
in the territory of the Attiwandaronks, and the towns of the latter afforded
safe refuge to fleeing parties of all the surrounding tribes.

The country of the Neutral Nation was south of Lake Ontario, and extended from the Genesee westward nearly to the shore of Huron, including the
Niagara river and a portion of the north coast of Lake Erie. The *Relations*
of the Jesuits describe them as living in twenty-eight villages, under the rule
of a noted war-chief named Souharissen. Their council fires were along the
Niagara, and their town nearest the Genesee but one day's journey from the
Senecas. They were superior to the Hurons in stature and strength, and the
men frequently went entirely naked. The early French missionaries who pen-
etrated their country found the Attiwandaronks exceedingly suspicious of all
intruders, but succeeded in visiting eighteen of their towns.

The neutrality so long maintained by these people was forcibly broken by
the Senecas in 1647. For some reason not well understood, the latter sud-
denly attacked the Attiwandaronks, and as early as 1651 had subdued the
entire nation. All old and feeble men and children were put to death and the
surviving warriors and women adopted by the conquerors. In time tribal dis-
tinctions were forgotten, and the descendants of the captive Attiwandaronks

---

[1] *League of the Iroquois*, p. 51.

became Senecas in heart and name. The destruction of the Neutral Nation, and the overthrow of the Eries in 1655, gave the conquerors control of all the country bordering the Genesee river, between the Alleghany mountains and Lake Ontario; and in after days the great valley of the Genesee was known as the "Vale of the Senecas." Within the historical period the council fire of the nation kindled at Genundawah has illumined the gloomy forest at Ga-o-sa-eh-ga-aah near Victor, gleamed brightly in the pleasant valley of the Genesee, and cast its expiring light over the shattered remnants of this once mighty people at Lake Erie; yet for nearly three centuries after Columbus kissed the ocean-laved sands of San Salvador, the Senecas held possession and control of the land originally occupied by them in the Genesee country, erected their rude cabins on its watercourses, roamed its hills and dales, hunted through its forest glades, lived, fought and died brave, lordly masters of the soil inherited from their fathers, whose crumbling bones the plow of the pale face still upturns as the seasons of harvest recur.

CHAPTER V.

Water Trails — Terminology of the Genesee River and Irondequoit Bay — Little Beard's Town — Casconchagon — The Jesuits — Indian Expedition up the Genesee — The Mouth of the Genesee Practically at Irondequoit Bay — Early Maps — Teoronto Bay — Mississauge Indians the Last at Irondequoit.

ALL tradition of ancient migrations of the red men refer to some navigable water as the route over which they came, or went. The canoe was the earliest known conveyance of primitive man, and water was his favorite highway. Says Bancroft: "Emigration by water suits the genius of savage life; a gulf, a strait, the sea intervening between islands, divides less than the matted forest. To the uncivilised man no path is free but the sea, the lake and the river."[1]

The Iroquois entered New York from Lake Ontario. Their first journey was down the Mohawk and Hudson to the ocean, and their return up those rivers was accomplished in canoes.[2] In the near vicinity of the numerous lakes and streams of the interior were founded their earliest and largest settlements. The Genesee has ever been the principal natural water highway of Western New York, and for unnumbered centuries the light crafts of the natives have glided over this limpid trail on missions of peace and war. Constituting, as it

[1] *History of the United States*, vol. III., p. 317.
[2] *Legends of the Senecas*, by J. W. Sanborn, p. 11. In his narration of this migration, the great historian of the Senecas informed Rev. Mr. Sanborn that the people carried their canoes from one stream, or body of water, to another.

did, the original western boundary line of their territory, the river was well known to all the Iroquois nations. After the destruction of Gaosaehgaah by DeNonville, the Senecas occupied the Genesee valley, and in early colonial times their great town was near the confluence of the river and Canaseraga creek. At a subsequent period it was located near the present site of Cuyler-ville. One hundred years ago it bore the name of its chief, Little Beard. It was termed the Chinesee Castle, and in the old colonial records, of a date prior to Little Beard's occupation of the place, it is variously mentioned as Chen-us-sio, Chin-as-si-o, Chen-nu-assio, Chin es-se, Chin-os-sio, Chen-ne-se-co, Gen-is-hau, Gen-nis-he-yo, Gen-ish-a-u, Jen-nis-see-ho, Gen-ne-se-o, Gen-ne-see. The apparent discrepancy in the orthography of the word is easily explained when it is understood that every tribe of the Six Nations conversed in its own dialect, and that each tribe in the same nation possessed peculiarities of speech not common in other tribes. All Indian names, either of persons or of places, are significant of some supposed quality, appearance, or local situation, in brief are descriptive, and the tribes denominated persons and places in conformity to such quality, etc., in their own dialects.

The Indians had no permanent names for places, and before Little Beard's time the town was known only by its descriptive title of Gen-nis-he-o, the pronunciation of which was varied by the different tribes, according to the peculiarities of each dialect, yet all signifying the same thing substantially — to-wit, Gen-ish-a-u, "shining-clear-opening;" Chen-ne-se-co, "pleasant-clear-opening;" Gen-ne-see, "clear-valley" or "pleasant-open-valley;" Gen-nis-he-yo, "beautiful valley." This term was local and originally applied only to that portion of the river near Cuylerville then occupied by the Chen-nus-se-o Indians, but owing to the large size of the town, and its important location, the name Genesee gradually displaced all others and became the general designation of the entire river. Ga-hun-da is a common noun signifying a "river" or "creek." The Iroquois usually affixed it to the proper name of a stream, as Gen-is-he-yo Ga-hun-da or Genesee river.

The native name of the lower Genesee first mentioned by early writers is Casconchagon. According to Bruyas, a Jesuit missionary to the Five Nations, the literal meaning of the name by which the Mohawks and Onondagas distinguished the Genesee river is "at the fall," Gascons-age. It is derived from Gasco, "something alive in the kettle;" as if the waters were agitated by some living animal.[1] The Seneca name is Gaskosago. Morgan renders the interpretation "Under the Falls," and in his table exhibiting the dialectical variations of the language of the Iroquois, as illustrated in their geographical names, gives the inflective differences of the name, as pronounced by the Six Nations.[2]

[1] N. Y. Col. Mss., IX., 1092.
[2] League of the Iroquois, p. 394.

In the Jesuit *Relations* for 1662-3, Father Lallemant says that in the month of April (1663) eight hundred Iroquois warriors proceeded from the western end of Lake Ontario to a fine river resembling the St. Lawrence, but free from falls and rapids, which they descended one hundred leagues to the principal Andastogue village, which was found to be strongly fortified, and the aggressors were repulsed. In a note, embodying the above statement, on page 37 of *Early Chapters of Cayuga History*, by Charles Hawley, D. D., General John S. Clark says: "This route appears to have been through the Genesee river, to Canaseraga creek, thence up that stream and by a short portage to Canisteo river, and thence down the Canisteo, Chemung and Susquehanna rivers to the fort. This route is indicated on the earlier maps, as one continuous river, flowing from Lake Ontario."

In the map prepared by General Clark, for Rev. Dr. Hawley's work, the route pursued by the expedition is represented as extending from the head of Irondequoit bay southwesterly to the Genesee river, and doubtless had reference to the portage trail (described in chapter VI.) between Irondequoit landing and Red creek ford. Though the route by the lower Genesee and around the falls, on the present site of Rochester, was several miles less than by the Irondequoit portage, the Iroquois appear to have preferred the latter course as the better known and established road. On Guy Johnson's map of the country of the Six Nations, in 1771, this trail is plainly indicated as the "Indian path to the lake," and many circumstances within the knowledge of the present writer induce a belief that in Indian times Irondequoit bay was considered the the practical mouth of the Genesee river. In certain old records the names Casconchagon and Irondequoit are occasionally applied equally to river and bay, as though having reference to one locality, but the former appears to have been least known, and it is quite certain that, to all the vast country of the Senecas, Irondequoit bay was the northern outlet. Its geographical position on the southern shore of Lake Ontario, midway between Chouaguen (Oswego) and Niagara, rendered it the most convenient and important place, in a military view, in the Genesee country. It was the objective point of all expeditions, peaceful or warlike, to and from the Senecas, and from its headwaters trails ran to every part of the Iroquois territory, connecting with others to all parts of the continent.

From the shadow of grim old woods near its shores and dense thickets of matted vines concealing its numerous dells, the glittering eyes of savage sentinels kept watch o'er the blue expanse of Ontario for expected friends and foes. Under its pine-mantled cliffs the Indian chieftains rendezvoused their navies of birchen bark, and reckoned their numbers on belts of wampum. Around its borders echoed the "shrill yell of barbarian hordes," and the deep thunder of the pale-faces' cannon. Palisaded fortifications of red and white men have guarded the narrow passages at either extremity of the bay, and fleets of both races battled on the lake within shot of its entrance. Great armies of savage and civilised nations have occupied its broad sand-beach, sought refuge within its sheltering headlands and marched their serried columns over its tabled elevations. Every point and nook about the grand old bay has its thrilling history; yet few among the thousands who daily roam the shady groves of Irondequoit in summer, gaining health and strength in every draught of the pure lake breeze, know aught of the stirring, events of by-gone days enacted on these very grounds.

The first mention of Irondequoit bay, found in the *Documents Relating to the Colonial History of New York*, is that of Rev. Jean de Lamberville, a Jesuit missionary to the Five Nations, in a letter written at or near Onondaga, July 13th, 1684, to M. de la Barre, governor of Canada. Therein the reverend father refers to an expected visit of the French official to Kan-ia-tare-on-ta-quoat. The name, as thus given by De Lamberville, is from the Iroquois, or Mohawk, dialect, and signifies, literally, "an opening into, or from, a lake;" an inlet or bay, from Kaniatare, "a lake," and hontontogonan, "to open."[1] Marshall says the Seneca name is O-nyiu-da-on-da-gwat, "it turns out or goes aside."[2] Like all Indian names of places, it is descriptive, and refers to the prominent, or peculiar feature of the locality to which it is applied, and the fact that the south shore of Ontario is indented with several large bays which must have been equally well known to the natives indicates the superior importance of Irondequoit in their estimation, as the bay of all. Evidence of this is found in early maps of the Lake Ontario region.

The earliest known map of this part of the country was published in 1632, by Champlain. The great explorer places a large bay on the south shore of Lake Ontario in the exact location of Irondequoit, but omits the name. The Jesuits' map, published in 1664, represents Irondequoit bay and spells it "Andiatarontaouat." Vangondy's map, published in Paris in 1773, renders it "Ganientaoaguat." Upon the great map of Franquelin, hydrographer to the king, at Quebec, "drawn in 1688, by order of the governor and intendant of New France, from sixteen years' observations of the author," Irondequoit bay appears as "Gan-ni-a-tare-on-toquat," differing slightly in orthography, yet identical with the name mentioned by De Lamberville a few years before.

A conclusive proof of the great importance of this bay in the view of past generations is found in the fact that it still bears the native name by which it was distinguished at the advent of the whites, over two and a half centuries ago. The dissimilarity of tribal pronunciation, and orthographic variations are illustrated in the following list collated from many sources: Kan-ia-tare-on-to-guoat, Ganni-a-tare-on-to-guoat, Can ia-ter-un-de-quat, Adia-run-da-quat, Onia-da-ron-da-quat, On-gui-da-onda quoat, Eu-taun-tu-quet, Neo-da-on-

[1] *N. Y. Col. Mss.*, IX., 261.

[2] *DeNonville's Expedition*, by O. H. Marshall, in *Collections of New York Historical Society*, part second, p. 176.

da-quat, Tjer-on-da-quat, The-ne-on-de-quat, Tic-run-de-quat, The-ron-de-
quot, Tic-ron-de-quat, Tie-ron-te-quet, Tis-o-ron-de-quat, Ty-ron-de-quot,
Tic-rond-quit, O-ron-do-kott, Run-di-cutt, Ge-run-de-gutt, Je-ron-do-kat,
Je-ron-de-quet, Je-ron-de-quate, Jeron-de-kat, Jar-ron-di-gat, Qron-do-quat,
Iron-de-gatt, Iron-de-katt, Iron-de-quat, Iron-de-quot, Iron-de-quoit.

In Spafford's *Gazetteer of New York*, published in 1824, that author says
the Indians called it Teoronto (bay), a sonorous and purely Indian name, too
good to be supplanted by such vulgarisms as Gerundegut, or Irondequoit.
The Indians pronounce the name Tche-o-ron-tok, its signification being "where
the waves breathe and die," or "gasp and die." Spafford was the first author
to make this assertion. No mention of the name Teoronto, in connection
with Irondequoit bay, can be found elsewhere than in his work previous to its
issue in 1824. His information was derived from a correspondent in Rochester, whose only knowledge of the matter was obtained by questioning Indians
then living on the Ridge — or Oswego — trail, about one mile east of the bay,
in the town of Webster.[1] They were not Senecas — the last of that nation
having removed to reservations about 1798-9 — but Mississauges. The tribe
is now settled on Rice lake, in Canada, and as late as 1853-4 parties crossed
Lake Ontario in canoes to fish and hunt at Irondequoit bay. Doctor Peter
Crow and other native Mississauges still visit their white friends at Irondequoit. The name Teoronto was accepted by English writers, and is occasionally revived in foreign guide books. Marshall tells us that the word is not
Seneca but Mohawk, and its true signification "a place where there is a jam
of floodwood."[2]

CHAPTER VI.

Local Trails of the Genesee — Indian Fords, Towns and Fortifications — Butler's Rangers — Indian Spring — Sacrifice of the White Dog — Flint Quarry — Sgoh-sa-is-thah — Portage Trails —
Irondequoit Landing — The Tories' Retreat — Indian Salt Springs — Ancient Mounds.

WHILE the march of civilisation had advanced beyond the Genesee to the
north and west, the hunting-grounds of the Senecas were still in their
primitive state, and the cycle of a century is not yet complete since the white
man came into actual possession of the land and became acquainted with its
topographical features. To the pale-faced adventurer of the seventeenth century to whom all this vast territory was an unexplored blank, viewing the land

[1] Old settlers on Irondequoit bay, Amos Knapp, Isaac Drake and others, inform me that they
knew the Webster Indians well, and the latter possessed neither knowledge nor tradition respecting
the ancient name and history of the bay,

[2] O. H. Marshall, in *Collections of N. Y. Hist. Society*, part second, p. 176.

from his birchen canoe on Lake Ontario, the bays, rivers and larger creeks presented the only feasible routes by which it could be entered and traversed, yet, once within its borders, the hardy explorer found the country marked by an intricate net-work of foot paths which spread in every direction. These dark wood lanes unknown to civilised man, their soil heretofore pressed only by the feet of Indians and wild beasts, will ever be known in history as the "trails of the Genesee." They were the highways and by-ways of the native inhabitants, the channels of communication between nations, tribes and scattering towns, in which there was a never-ceasing ebb and flow of humanity.

The origin of these trails and the selection of the routes pursued were natural results of the every-day necessities and inclinations of the nomadic race first inhabiting the land, and time had gradually fashioned the varying interests of successive generations into a crude system of general thoroughfares to which all minor routes led. To find the beginning and end of these grand trails one might traverse the continent in a fruitless search, for, like the broader roads of the present white population, many of which follow the old trail courses, the beaten paths extended from ocean to ocean, from the southern point of Patagonia to the country of the Eskimos, where they were lost in the ever-shifting mantle of snow covering the land of ice — and the trails of the Genesee were but a local division of the mighty complication.

In general appearance these roads did not differ in any particular from the ordinary woods or meadow path of the present day. They were narrow and winding, but usually connected the objective points by as direct a course as natural obstacles would permit. In the general course of a trail three points were carefully considered — first, seclusion; second, directness, and, third, a dry path. The trail beaten was seldom over fifteen inches broad, passing to the right or left of trees or other obstacles, around swamps and occasionally over the apex of elevations, though it generally ran a little one side of the extreme top, especially in exposed situations. Avoiding open places save in the immediate neighborhood of towns and camps, it was universally shaded by forest trees. A somber silence, now and then interrupted by the notes of birds or the howling of beasts, reigned along these paths.[1] Fallen trees and logs were never removed, the trail was either continued over or took a turn around them. The Indians built no bridges, small streams were forded or crossed on logs, while rivers and lakes were ferried on rafts or in canoes.

The main trail of the Iroquois extended from Hudson, on the Hudson river below Albany, westwardly to Buffalo, crossing the Genesee at Cannawaugus — now Avon. From Canandaigua lake a branch ran northwest to the head of Irondequoit bay, then to the Genesee falls, and along the lake ridge to the Niagara river at Lewiston. This was the grand line of communication between the Five Nations, and the ultimate destination of every other trail in the pres-

---

ent state of New York. Along its silent course the swiftest runners of the Iroquois bore their messages of peace or war with a speed and physical endurance incredible. Morgan says : —

"Whenever the sachems of a nation desired to convene the grand council of the Iroquois league, they sent out runners, to the nation nearest, with a belt of wampum. This belt announced that on a certain day thereafter, at such a place, and for such and such purposes (mentioning them), a council of the league would assemble. If the message originated with the Senecas it reached the Cayugas first, as the nation located nearest upon the line of trail. The Cayugas then notified the Onondagas, they the Oneidas, and these the Mohawks ; the reverse being the order when the message originated in the east. Each nation within its own confines spread the information far and wide; and thus, in a space of time astonishingly brief, intelligence of the council was heralded from one extremity of their country to the other. If the subject was calculated to arouse a deep feeling of interest, one common impulse from the Hudson to the Niagara, and from the St. Lawrence to the Susquehanna, drew the people toward the council fire ; sachems, chiefs and warriors, women, and even children, deserted their hunting grounds and woodland seclusions, and literally flocked to the place of council."[1]

Their wandering, hunter life and habit of intent observation rendered the Iroquois familiar with every foot of land in their territory, enabling them to select the choicest locations for abode. Towns were frequently moved from place to place, new trails worn and old ones abandoned to stray hunters and wild animals. Trails leading to or along the edge of water were usually permanent. Hardly a stream but bore its border line of trail upon either bank. From the shore of Lake Ontario to the headwaters of the Genesee, trails followed every curve of the river as closely as natural obstacles would permit, and branches led up the sides of tributary creeks.

Trails converged on the Genesee in the vicinity of Rochester at two places, the ridge north of the lower falls, and the rapids some eighty rods below the mouth of Red creek. The passage of the river north of the lower falls was effected in canoes or on rafts ; in the absence of either or both, the aboriginal traveler plunged into the water and stemmed the strong current with his brawny arms. Before the white man obstructed its channel with dams the Genesee was one continuous rapid from Red creek to the south line of the present Erie canal aqueduct. An Indian ford existed at a shallow place near the immediate line of the present race-dam, between the jail and weigh-lock, but was never in such general use as the upper ford below Red creek, where the river could be more easily and safely crossed by footmen.

The great trail coming west from Canandaigua on the present route of the Pittsford road divided a few rods east of Allen's creek. The main trail turned to the north over a low ridge, across the present farm of the venerable Charles M. Barnes[2] and down a gully to Allen's creek. The ford was exactly at the

---

[1] *League of the Iroquois*, p. 110.

[2] No resident of Monroe county is more thoroughly interested in its aboriginal history than Charles M. Barnes. His admirable knowledge of colonial and pioneer history, and remarkable memory of

arch through which the waters now pass under the great embankment of the New York Central railroad. Following the west bank to a point where the creek turned directly to the right, the trail left the stream and curving gradually to the west along the base of a high bluff ran up a narrow gully to the table-land. Taking a northwest course from this point it passed the brick residence of D. McCarthy, crossed a trail running to the fishing resort on Irondequoit creek and at the distance of one hundred rods again curved to the west along a short slope, striking the line of the present road on the farm of Judge Edmund Kelley. In the side of this slope were numerous springs near which the Indians frequently camped. When the ground was first plowed many Indian relics were found, and also evidences of a former occupation by some large body of white men. At least two bushels of bullets were discovered in one spot, and numerous other indications of the presence of an army.

From these springs a trail ran directly north half a mile and turned east down the hillside to the famous Indian landing on Irondequoit creek Along this road between the springs and landing was located the famed Tryon's Town, of Gerundegut, founded by Judge John Tryon about 1798. From Tryon's Town the main trail continued its northwest course to the Thomas road, some rods north of University avenue. From that point the present (old Thomas) road leading to the cobble-stone school-house on Culver street, and thence to Norton street, runs on the old trail. Leaving Norton street a short distance east of Goodman, the path crossed a swamp to Hooker's cemetery. The ground in front of Mr. Hooker's residence is said to have been the site of a very ancient fortification. Following the north edge of the elevation the trail crossed North avenue to the Culver farm opposite, and can still be traced through the grove of forest trees to the former location of a large Indian settlement on the sand knolls,[1] half a mile west. From this town the course was due west down the side of Spring brook to the Ridge mounds and Brewer's landing on the Genesee river.

East avenue is located upon the general route of the second trail from Allen's creek westward. It divided near Union street, the principal path turning slightly to the south and ending at the ford near the weighlock. The branch crossed Main street near the liberty pole and struck the river trail in the vicinity of Franklin and North St. Paul streets. Indian huts were scattered about the bluff in that vicinity until 1819.

A trail came from Caledonia springs east by way of Mumford, Scottsville, Chili and Gates to Red creek ford in South Rochester. This was the general thoroughfare from the Indian towns near the Canaseraga creek to the lower

early events in the vicinity of Rochester, have proved invaluable aids in the collection of many facts herein presented.

[1] In a conversation held with David Forest on this very ground, in 1854, Oliver Culver stated that in 1796 he arrived at Irondequoit landing in a canoe, and came over the trail described to this town, where he traded with the Indians. It was from them that he received his information regarding the large skeletons discovered at the mouth of Irondequoit bay.

Genesee and Lake Ontario. It was down this trail that Butler's rangers fled, after the massacre of Boyd and Parker at Little Beard's Town in 1779, on their way to the mouth of the river.

A path seldom used during the later Seneca occupation ran north from Red creek ford in the general direction of Genesee street, to the head of Deep hollow, around which it curved to the Lake avenue trail. From this path a second came north from the rapids over the course of Plymouth avenue to a spot called Indian spring (near the corner of Spring street and Spring alley in rear of the First Presbyterian church), and followed the little spring creek northeast to the vicinity of Central avenue and Mill street. This trail branched near Atkinson street, the branch running eastward to the ford near the present jail. From this ford a path ran directly to Indian spring, in the vicinity of which the wigwams of the natives were occasionally set up. It was at the southern extremity of the ridge lying west of this spring that the Senecas made their last sacrifice of the white dog. Lewis H. Morgan is authority for the statement that this ceremony was performed on the ground now occupied by W. S. Kimball's residence on the south side of Troup street, between Eagle street and Caledonia avenue. A third trail turned north from the jail ford and connected with the Plymouth avenue trail near Central avenue, continuing north to Deep hollow, where it was joined by the Genesee street trail. At the present Ridge road on the boulevard the trail separated; the main path running west on the ridge to Lewiston, and the other to the lake shore. The summit of the hill over which Lake avenue passes, near the present residence of Charles J. Burke, was once the site of a large Indian town, and all the slope and low ground east of that place to the river and north to Hanford's landing, was used for camping purposes. There were numerous springs along this hillside, and the Indians obtained flint from a quarry on the edge of the bluff[1] near the river end of Frauenberger avenue. Numerous little heaps of flint chips, half-finished and broken arrow-heads, and other weapons of stone were found in the woods of that locality by the early settlers. Upon these grounds the late Dr. Chester Dewey gathered many valuable relics of the stone age now in the Smithsonian institution.

The waters of the springs mentioned once formed a short creek, the channel of which was parallel with and some rods west of the edge of the bluff. This channel is yet quite distinct and so straight as to suggest the idea of artificial origin. It emptied over the edge of the cliff into the great dell at Hanford's landing. At the upper end of this dell the waters of a larger stream, which has its source some miles westward, still dash recklessly over the cliff and hurry through the rocky passage below to join the river. Between these creeks, on land now owned by R. J. Smith, the ground takes the form of a low ridge, extending some distance southward from the cliff. The situation is grand

---

[1] *Pioneer Historical Collections.*

and the view down the river and over the water, some two hundred feet below, very pleasing. A great fortification once stood on this ridge, but when or by whom constructed history tells not. Over a century ago it was a mere heap of ruins. Squier says it consisted of a semi-circular embankment, the ends of which reached the very edge of the immense ravine, and had three narrow gate-ways placed at irregular intervals.[1] Every part of the embankment was obliterated long years ago, but its lines have been inferred by the quantities of relics found within certain sharply defined limits. It is a singular fact that no cemetery has been discovered in the vicinity of this place, the nearest burial-ground of the aborigines west of the Genesee, known to the writer, being some two miles distant.

There is a legend connected with some cliff near the lower falls of the Genesee river, and this may, possibly, be the spot. Stripped of the fanciful language in which the mythical narratives of the red man are usually clothed, it is a simple pathetic tale. 'Tis said that a pale-faced wanderer paddled up the river one summer's day, long years ago. He came alone directly to an Indian camp on the river side, and remained with the tribe. In time his native country and his people were forgotten in the happiness of loving, and being loved by, a beautiful forest maiden. They were married in the Indian fashion, and the days passed away like moments in their lodge "near the singing cataract." One day a strange canoe, filled with white men, came up the Genesee in search of the pale-faced wanderer, who proved to be an exiled chieftain (nobleman) of France. His friends came to carry him back to honor and fortune, but his heart was in the wildwoods and he refused to go. Then they sought to compel him, but, clasping his Indian wife in his arms, the exile rushed to the brink of a great cliff where the rock rose straight up above the water, and, springing far out over the precipice, the two were crushed and mangled on the rocks below. Tradition has failed to preserve the names of the white brave and his dusky bride, or identify the place of their death. The brief description of locality answers equally well to the bluff opposite the Glen House, or this dell at Hanford's landing.

From the top of the cliff within the limits of the old fort a stone can be cast to the water's edge at Hanford's landing below. From the landing a path ran along the water at the base of the bluff, up the river to the lower falls. At the spot now called Buell's landing, directly opposite Brewer's landing, a path led up the face of the jutting rocks, reaching the table land in the vicinity of the flint quarry, and natives crossing the river often climbed this steep path in preference to the longer route by the lower landing. The first white settlers in this vicinity (Gideon King and others) widened a path leading up the great sloping bank from the old Indian landing north, to a wagon road. In 1798 Eli Granger laid the keel of the Jemima, a schooner of forty tons and the first

---

[1] *Aboriginal Monuments of New York,* p. 58.

American vessel built on the Genesee (some say the first built near Lake Ontario), at the foot of this road ; the landing, then called King's, now Hanford's,
became the lake port, and there the steamer Ontario first touched the river
bank when she commenced her trips in 1817. From the landing a second path
curved up the little promontory on the north side of the dell, and extended
around the edge of the cliff to the old fort. From that place it ran up the
creek to the main or Ridge trail, which it crossed some distance west of the
present boulevard. Continuing along the north bank of the creek to the farm
of Samuel Truesdale, where the giant skeleton was exhumed in 1878, it turned
west along the mountain ridge, running straight to a spring on the present farm
of George H. Lee. Indians came upon this creek and camped in Mr. Truesdale's chestnut grove until 1853.

At the rapids in South Rochester the river passes over a ledge of limestone, and before the dam was constructed the channel was very shallow some
sixty rods above and below. On the east bank a flat extended from Red creek
north around the base of Oak hill. It was eaten away by the current long
years ago, but it originally constituted the the east-side landing of the ford.
The west end of Elmwood avenue strikes the river just south of the upper edge
of the old ford. In early pioneer days there were two or three good springs
in the bank of a small creek which entered the river at that point. A pre-
historic town, covering all the surface of Oak hill, once existed there. Stone
relics were found on every foot of the ground from the feeder dam to Red creek,
by the early settlers. In their anxiety to distance Sullivan's soldiers, Butler's
men rid themselves of everything possible at this ford. Ammunition and arms
were buried in the ground near the springs and concealed in hollow trees in
the vicinity. In 1816 Mr. Boughton found ninety-six pounds of bullets in
the bottom of a rotten stump, and several other discoveries of bullets, bars of
lead, etc., have been made by various parties.

From the springs at the ford the trail ran northeast to the corner of Indian
Trail and First avenues in Mount Hope cemetery. At that point it divided,
one branch turning sharply to the left, directly up the slope and north over
the top of section G to the present Indian Trail avenue, which it entered and
thence followed the ridge straight to a spot in front of George Ellwanger's residence, continuing down Mount Hope avenue, South and North St. Paul streets
to Brewer's landing. From the latter place it ran near the edge of the high
bank to Lake Ontario. On the farm of Daniel Leake traces of an Indian town
and burial ground have been discovered and the old path can yet be followed
in places through the woods north of the "rifle range." An ancient fortification stood near the ford of a brook which rises in the little vale southeast of
Rattlesnake point. It was the ruins of this fort for which Mr. Squier searched
in vain about 1848. The Seneca ferrying-place across the river was at the
terminus of the trail at about the same location as the present upper ferry at

Charlotte. In the brush and woods on the east bank at this point Butler's rangers sought refuge while waiting for the tory Walker to return from Fort Niagara with boats for their removal. The log house afterward occupied by Walker stood a few feet southeast of the angle in the present road where it turns west across the swamp at the ferry. Stone pestles, arrow-heads, bullets, etc., have been found in the vicinity in considerable numbers by Jerome Manning and other old settlers.

From the corner of Indian Trail and First avenues in Mount Hope cemetery the south branch of the trail, coming from Red creek ford, passed a few rods east to a beautiful spring in the side of the present artificial pond. Curving slightly northward it divided, one path following the general course of Stanley street and Highland avenue along the southern base of the hills to the corners north of Cobb's brick-yard on Monroe avenue; the other branch running directly to the summit of the hills near the water-works reservoir, and east over the top of Pinnacle hill, joining the first path near the corners. From that place the course was directly east to the riffle on Irondequoit creek some distance above the dug-way mills. This riffle was a noted resort of the Indians who went there from the upper Genesee to fish. It was known to the Senecas as Sgoh-sa-is-thah. The meaning of the word is "the swell dashes against the precipice," referring to the fact that a heavy swell sometimes beats against the ledge over which the fall pours. Springs still exist in the bank near the riffle where the Indians camped. From this fishing ground a large open path ran directly south over the hills to the Pittsford road, and thence to Honeoye. At its crossing of the New York Central railroad at the "sand-cut" east of the Allen's creek embankment, an Indian burial ground was located. During the excavation of a part of this hill, about 1876, human remains were exhumed, among which were several skeletons of unusual size, one exceeding seven feet in length. Numberless relics of stone, rusty knives and fragments of firearms were picked up by the workmen, Dennis Callahan securing a small flat-iron bearing the figure of a spread eagle. East of this trail, between the cemetery and the Pittsford road, quantities of stone relics have been found, indicating the site of a pre-historic town. West of this site is located the great cairn of limestones, supposed to have been heaped up by people preceding the Indians.

There were two Indian roads known as the portage trails. The first has been described as the Mount Hope avenue and St. Paul street route, over which canoes and baggage were transported between Red creek and Brewer's landing. This route was followed by the Indians long after Rochester was settled by the whites, and Phederus Carter, James Stone and other pioneer boys often assisted their Indian friends to carry canoes over this path.

The grand portage trail diverged from the Mount Hope avenue path near Clarissa street, ran along the ridge south of and parallel with Gregory street to

South avenue, thence straight to Oliver Culver's old homestead, corner of Culver street and East avenue. Passing a few rods east of the house the trail-route was down the north road east to the landing on Irondequoit creek. This was the general highway between the upper Genesee and Irondequoit bay, to which reference has been made in chapter V. Some years ago an aged Seneca was asked to describe the route of this trail between the Genesee river and Irondequoit landing. Raising his hand and cleaving the air with a direct forward blow the Indian replied: "Straight as the arrow flies, runs the carrying-path." A verification of this assertion may be found on any map of Monroe county showing the following points: Mount Hope avenue and Clarissa street, South avenue and Grand street, East avenue and the Culver road and the landing on Irondequoit creek. A line extending from the first to the last would pass in as nearly a direct course through the intermediate points as the original form of the ground would admit. From South avenue to East avenue the trail ran over a section of low ground which extended southward to the base of the Pinnacle range of hills, and was known as the "bear swamp."

A huge dome-shaped hill fills the Irondequoit valley directly opposite the old Indian landing-place so often mentioned. The creek hugs the west bank at the landing and sweeps around to the southeast in a great semi-circle called "the ox-bow," leaving a crescent-shaped flat at the southern base of this island hill. When the surrounding slopes were covered with forest trees this flat formed a pleasant and secluded retreat, which could only be reached over the landing trail or by crossing the creek, which is very deep in that vicinity. After leaving Red creek ford Butler's rangers separated on Mount Hope, one party proceeding down the Mount Hope avenue trail to the mouth of the Genesee, the other going east to Irondequoit landing and the ox-bow flat, which appears to have been a well known and favorite resort of the tories. From this hiding-place they made their way over the town of Irondequoit to the mouth of the Genesee river, where they remained in the brush and the woods several days, not daring to build a fire or make the least noise, lest Sullivan's avenging forces should discover and annihilate them. Walker had been sent from Caledonia springs to Niagara for boats, and when he finally arrived in the Genesee the rangers were nearly famished. After one ravenous meal they embarked for Niagara and Oswego, and the lower Genesee was rid of all the murderous gang save Walker, who, remaining as a British spy, built a cabin near the ferrying-place.

The west side of the island hill, facing Irondequoit landing, has yielded to nature's erosive forces, and a charming inclined valley extends from the landing to the very eastern limit of the hilltop, which was once connected with the high land east by a narrow ridge. From the landing the old trail course was up this valley to the elevated table land opposite. Running some distance east to avoid the tremendous gulfs reaching back from the bay, it turned north, ending on the sand-bar at the mouth of Irondequoit bay. From the landing to Lake Ontario every rod of ground is historical. When the farms of Henry Smith and Edson Welcher, just north of the float-bridge road, were settled, an Indian cemetery was discovered. There were two hundred grave-mounds arranged in rows, over which grew oak trees fully eighteen inches in diameter. In the woods near at hand great corn-hills were plainly to be seen, and the Indians had a landing-place on Plum Orchard point, immediately below.

A second trail turned east to the ridge, along which it continued to Sodus and Oswego. It was known to the Senecas as Ne-aga Wa-a-gwen, or Ontario foot-path. The village last occupied by Seneca Indians in Webster was located on the ridge near this path, about one mile east of the bay, and the latter-day Mississauges camped on the same ground. Their landing was on the bay, at the foot of the ridge. In a hollow north of the landing H. M. Hames discovered twelve skeletons lying in a circle, like the spokes of a wheel, with their feet to the center, where were deposited a number of rude stone weapons, probably arms of the buried warriors. One of these relics, an immense spear-head of flint, is in possession of the writer. It is an interesting fact that while iron weapons, beads and other evidences of association with the whites are occasionally found in graves of the natives on the high land about Rochester, burial-places in hollows or ravines usually contain relics of the stone age only. A mound which was very prominently located on the bluff north of Dunbar hollow was opened by the early residents, who obtained a great number of stone weapons, mostly tomahawks and skull-crackers.

A large fort once occupied the ground just north of the ridge at the intersection of the sand-bar trail. This work is mentioned by Macauley, but Squier failed to locate it in 1848.[1] DeNonville does not appear to have observed it in 1687, and it was undoubtedly very ancient. Stone arrow-heads discovered there are quite large and broad. Arrow-heads of the same description are found in a dell on the Victor trail. From the old fort a trail ran northeast to a salt-spring located about one and a half miles east of the bay. The Indians came from Gardeau, Mount Morris, Moscow, Geneseo, Lima, Avon and Cannawaugus to make salt at this spring, camping in the woods between it and Irondequoit bay. The tory Walker and an old Seneca chief from Moscow were the last to use it, and in 1788-9 they covered the spring over. They disclosed its location in confidence to three or four white friends, Asa Dunbar being of the number. He revealed it to Wm. H. Penfield, and the latter to Jarvis M. Hatch, from whom the present writer obtained the following quaint directions to effect its re-discovery: "In a large gorge half a mile from the lake shore take a runway to a point one-fourth of a mile southwest of the gorge. The spring is near some trees in a cultivated field, entirely covered over and effectually concealed. I have been to it in 1860." There was another spring in Dunbar hol-

---

[1] *Aboriginal Monuments*, p. 58.

low, which is so called from the fact that Asa Dunbar, an early settler of gigantic strength, frequented the place to manufacture salt. The process was very simple, the brine being boiled in a "three-pail kettle."

Two mounds once occupied the hilltop south of the Sea Breeze hotel on the west side of Irondequoit bay. Their former location was pointed out to the writer in 1880 by Charles M. Barnes and Amos Knapp. The mounds were from twenty to thirty-five feet east of north of the present wooden "observatory." Squier says they were small, the largest not exceeding five feet in height. Upon excavation he found they had been previously disturbed, and his examination resulted in the discovery of a few fragments of bone, charcoal, pottery and arrow-heads.[1] Old settlers inform me that Wm. H. Penfield opened these mounds about 1817. He obtained many curious things, including sword scabbard-bands of silver, belt buckles, belt and hat ornaments and other articles of military dress. Directly east of these mounds is a deep gully, now crossed by two rustic bridges. The Indian canoe landing was at the mouth of this gully, where a fine spring furnished good water. A trail came up the hill from the sand-bar west of the mounds along the edge of the gully to its beginning. A few rods east of this point was a burial-place where Indian remains are still found. The gully or landing trail united with the other, ran southwest to the ridge in the vicinity of the Forest House, and due south to the west end of the float-bridge road, where it joined the trail already described, leading to the camping-ground on Judge Kelley's farm and onward through the Allen's creek "defile" to the Pittsford road. This was the main trail, west of the bay, from Lake Ontario to Irondequoit landing, Victor and Honeoye creek, and DeNonville marched down this path from Allen's creek on his return to the lake.

The small island on the west side of Irondequoit bay, upon which the Schneider House stands, is of artificial origin. It was originally of ellipsoidal form, ninety feet long, thirty-two wide and seventeen high. In his preparations to build, Mr. Schneider lowered the whole island to within two feet of the surface of the water, first removing a dead oak tree about fifteen inches through, which stood on the very top of the elevation. The mound was composed of alternate layers of sand and clay so distinctly marked as to attract attention. In the bottom of the exact center, fifteen feet below the surface, Mr. Schneider unearthed about one bushel of hand-worked stones consisting of arrow and spear heads, knives, tomahawks of various shapes, skull-crackers, war-club heads, fish-net weights, skin-dressers, finishers, etc. Some of these articles were beautiful specimens of polished-stone work and nearly all above the average size usually found in this vicinity. The construction of this mound cost a vast amount of labor, and the object is conjectural. It marked the entrance to a small bay which undoubtedly constituted a fine harbor extending

---

[1] *Aboriginal Monuments,* p. 57.

back into a great valley. It is a secluded locality, immense forest trees still standing about the shore, but was once frequented by the native inhabitants. A brawling stream curves through the valley bottom and enters the little bay, which has become nearly impassable by the growth of rushes. A trail extended the whole length of the valley and the old path is yet quite distinct in places. It followed the original upward course of the stream to the north end of Culver street. A trail left the creek at the head of the valley and ran south across the float-bridge road some two miles to the Irondequoit creek landing and Genesee falls trail, which it crossed near the old Thomas road, and continued up the bank of a creek to the portage trail at Oliver Culver's old homestead on East avenue. Numberless side paths connected these principal trails at intervals, and threaded the forest in every direction to springs, deer-licks, and other places of interest to the native inhabitants. Other trails will be mentioned in their proper connections, but many interesting facts are omitted, enough having already been presented to prove that a numerous population occupied the territory of the lower Genesee long before the white man came upon its soil.

CHAPTER VII.

Early French Missions — Tsonnontouan — The Jesuit's Escape — La Salle at Irondequoit — Struggle between the French and English for Possession of the Lower Genesee Country.

THOUGH the Franciscan Le Caron is supposed to have passed through the Iroquois (Mohawk) country about 1616, *coureurs des bois* are known to have traded with tribes on the south shore of Ontario before De la Roche Dallion passed the winter of 1626–7 with the Neuters, the whites possessed no definite knowledge of Western New York or the water connections of Lake Ontario with the west, until 1640, when Brébeuf's mission to the Neuters perfected their knowledge of the Niagara river and Lake Erie. "Could we but gain the mastery of the shore of Ontario on the side nearest the abode of the Iroquois," the Jesuits said, "we could ascend by the St. Lawrence without danger, and pass free beyond Niagara, with a great saving of time and pains."

To accomplish this end the French bent all their energies. In the canoes of the traders, ofttimes preceding them, went the brave priests to plant the standard of the Roman church and extend the dominion of France, in the wilds of Western New York. With varying success they advanced from Onondaga westward until, in 1657, Chaumont preached the faith in the towns of the Senecas, but in two short years war between the French and Iroquois again drove

the missionaries to the northern shore of Ontario. In 1661 Le Moyne returned
to Onondaga, and several missions were re-established. In the fall of 1668 a
deputation of Seneca chiefs visited Montreal and requested the Jesuits to establish missions in their country, that the people might share all the advantages of
religion enjoyed by Iroquois nations to the east. In compliance with this
request Father Frémin was sent to Tsonnontouan, as the Genesee country was
then called by the French. The good priest arrived at his post of duty November 1st, and, taking up his abode at the same town wherein Chaumont had
preached, founded the mission of St. James. At that date the Senecas had
four large villages east of the Genesee river. Through the researches of O. H.
Marshall the location of these towns has been definitely fixed. The principal
village, at which Frémin resided, was situated on what is now termed Boughton hill, near Victor. The exact site is south of the railroad, on a farm owned
by R. B. Moore. Wentworth Greenhalp, who visited the town in 1677, describes its location and appearance under the name of Canagorah. Ten years
later DeNonville, who destroyed the place, mentions it in his official report by
its Mohawk designation of Ganangorah. In this effort to re-discover the site of
this town Marshall learned its correct Seneca name — Ga-o-sa-eh-ga-aah.[1]

Father Garnier, who had been stationed at Onondaga, joined Frémin in his
labors and established the mission of St. Michael at Gan-don-ga-rae, a small
village located on Mud creek, between three and four miles southeast of Victor,
where he remained several years. Bruyas, Pierron and other priests visited
these towns during the life of the missions, and the general route to and from
the Seneca villages appears to have been through Irondequoit bay. In 1683
Garnier was secretly informed of the intention of the French to make war
upon the Iroquois, and, hastening to Irondequoit landing, he was concealed and
escaped in a little barque belonging to the French government, which lay at
anchor there, trading with the natives.

August 10th, 1669, La Salle, the afterward noted French explorer, arrived
at the mouth of Irondequoit with seven canoes and twenty-four men, including
Dollier de Casson and Galinée, two priests of the seminary of St. Sulpice,
Montreal. They were accompanied by two other canoes bearing a party of
Senecas, who had wintered on the St. Lawrence and were now acting as guides.
La Salle's object in this visit was to obtain a guide to the Ohio river, that of
the priests the conversion of the natives. The party landed on the sand-
bar and were escorted to "Sonnontouan" or Gannagora by crowds of

---

[1] The etymology of this name was explained to Mr. Marshall in 1847 by Blacksmith, the principal
chief of the Senecas. He said the whole village was supplied by one spring, which issued from the
side of a hill. To procure water more conveniently the Indians made troughs or conductors of basswood bark, which, when stripped from the tree, curls readily into the proper shape, and with these
they conducted the water to a point where it could be caught in their vessels. The fact that this was
the only spring in the vicinity gave prominence to the use of the basswood bark, and hence, according
to the Indian custom, arose the name Ga-o-sa-eh-ga-aah, or "the basswood bark lies there." — O.
H. Marshall, in *DeNonville's Expedition*, p. 159.

savages. They remained with the Senecas one month, and failing to accomplish their purpose departed westward along the shore of Lake Ontario. During the following two years La Salle was upon the soil of Western New York many times, and undoubtedly explored every foot of the Genesee river from its mouth to Portage, in his efforts to discover the route to the Ohio and Mississippi. That he visited Irondequoit bay on several occasions is well known.

With their first faint knowledge of the interior of New York and the great lake region, the whites keenly appreciated the sagacity of the red men in their selection of Irondequoit bay as the general landing-place of the Senecas and harbor of the league, and recognised the important bearing its possession would have upon the steadily increasing interests of trade and future civilisation. With the French on the north, and the English and Dutch on the south and east, to all of whom the great lakes and streams presented the only practicable channels of communication with the west, the Iroquois country became the center of conflicting interests, and, simultaneously with the supremacy of the English in Eastern New York, came the struggle between that nation and the French for possession of the great lake region and control of the Indian trade. Niagara was the key to the western lakes, and Oswego and Irondequoit the ports through which all the costly loads of Indian goods and rich cargoes of furs must naturally pass to the west and east; for, though the French held possession of the St. Lawrence and had free access to Ontario, the journey thither was long and perilous, and Indian goods could be purchased in Albany and transported to Montreal at a less rate than they could be imported direct to that place from France,[1] while the trails of the Iroquois, which could be traveled from Albany to Irondequoit on horseback, and the watercourses of the interior of New York presented shorter, safer and more profitable routes for unrestricted traffic; hence the desire of the English to open the way to the west, and the endeavors of the French to obtain possession of Oswego, Irondequoit and Niagara, close them to the English and secure the Indian trade to the French colony of the St. Lawrence. Added to this was the natural enmity existing between the two nations and the jealous rivalry and inordinate greed for territorial possessions in the New world. Each nation claimed the Iroquois country, France by right of first discovery and occupation, England by virtue of conquest from the Dutch and treaty stipulations, and both enacted the monarchical role of paternal proprietorship, endeavoring to awe and control the various tribes by alternate threatenings and persuasion.

From the attack of Champlain on the Mohawks at Ticonderoga point in 1609, the Iroquois as a nation had maintained a relentless enmity toward the French, though a shadow of peace had occasionally been made and some hundreds of Indians enticed to Canada through the religious influence of French priests; on the other hand the Iroquois had steadily inclined to the English, who were their acknowledged friends and allies. Despairing of ultimate success by other means than force, the governors of Canada invaded the country of the Five Nations on several occasions with armies of colonists and Indian allies, but neither honors nor lasting benefits accrued to the French from these expeditions. In 1685 De la Barre was recalled to France and the marquis De-Nonville succeeded him as governor-general of Canada. Despite the influence of French missionaries in their midst, the Iroquois still barred the way to a free navigation of water highways leading to the west, insolently repudiated the authority of the French government, and openly avowed their friendship for the English, who were permitted to set up the British arms in several Iroquois villages.

CHAPTER VIII.[1]

DeNonville's Expedition — Treachery of the French Governor-General — Magnanimity of the Iroquois — French Army at Irondequoit — Execution of Marion — The Fort on the Sand-Bar — The March on Gannagaro — The Defiles, Ambuscade and Battle — Horrors of Indian Warfare — Cannibalism — Destruction of the Seneca Towns.

UPON assuming the reins of colonial government, DeNonville determined to break the power of the Iroquois and subdue their pride by an invasion of the Seneca settlements. To conceal his intentions the wily governor made overtures to the savages through the Jesuits stationed in their villages, and the summer of 1686 was spent in negotiations which terminated by the adoption of a resolution that both parties — French and Iroquois — should meet at Cataracouy,[2] to take measures for the conclusion of a general peace. Neither party placed confidence in the proposed peaceful measures, and the French had no intention of obtaining peace through treaty. During the entire summer De-Nonville was very anxious to lay up a store of provisions and munitions at Cataracouy in preparation for the next season's campaign, but was restrained from so doing through fear of alarming the Iroquois. Active preparations were instituted during the winter and spring of 1686-7. Fort Cataracouy — then a small redoubt — was placed in defensible condition, stocked with the necessary supplies, and the three small vessels on Lake Ontario secured for service.

June 12th, 1687, the French governor left Montreal for Cataracouy with an army consisting of eight hundred and thirty-two regular troops; nine hun-

---

[1] The material for this chapter is collated from the Colonial and Documentary Histories of New York ; the *Expedition of the Marquis DeNonville against the Senecas, in 1687*, by O. H. Marshall; *Discovery of the Great West*, by Francis Parkman ; Historical sketches in the Victor *Herald*, by J. W. Van Denburgh, and the writer's private journal.

[2] Kingston.

dred and thirty militia, over one hundred colonial scouts and four hundred Indians. Of this force M. de Callières was commander-in-chief, under the orders of the Marquis DeNonville, Chevalier de Vaudreuil, commander of the regulars, and General Sieur Duguay (Du Gue) commandant of the militia. The troops were formed into eight platoons of two hundred men each, the regulars under Captains D'Orvilliers, St. Cirg, de Troyes and Vallerennes, the militia under Captains Berthier, la Valterye, Grandville and Longueil Le Moynes. In the order of march a battalion of regulars succeeded one of militia, alternately. Six bateaux were assigned to each company, each boat carrying eight men, baggage and provisions, each captain having charge of twenty-four bateaux. The Indians served as guides and scouts and marched without order. The army arrived at Cataracouy July 1st, after a terribly laborious voyage up the rapids of the St. Lawrence, and engaged in preparations for the contemplated expedition. Two of the little vessels were loaded with supplies, and two large bateaux furnished with cannon and long guns to cover the troops while landing. The third vessel was sent to Niagara laden with provisions and ammunition for a party under Sieurs de Tonty, de la Durantaye and du Lhu (Du Luth), who had received instructions the previous summer to collect all the French, and Indian allies from the western woods, for this expedition. Orders were also forwarded by messenger for the reinforcements to meet Governor DeNonville at Irondequoit bay on a certain date.

Notwithstanding the warlike preparations of the French, which drew an official remonstrance from Governor Dongan of New York and excited the alarm of the Five Nations, DeNonville stoutly declared his pacific intentions, and, under a pretense of holding a great council for the ratification of peace, induced the Jesuit missionaries to decoy to Canada a number of Iroquois. Upon their arrival at Cataracouy these people were made prisoners and fifty of the men, including several sachems and chiefs, sent to Montreal, in company with certain other Indians who had been captured while fishing on the river during the upward voyage of the French army. *By order of his most Christian Majesty, the king, these proud warriors were shipped to France as slaves for the royal galleys.* When news of DeNonville's infamous act reached the Onondagas, "among whom Father Lamberville was then residing as a missionary," says Marshall, " the chiefs immediately assembled in council and sending for the father related the above transaction with all the energy which a just indignation could arouse, and, while he expected to feel the full effects of the rage which he saw depicted in every countenance, one of the old men unexpectedly addressed to him the following remarkable language, as related by Lamberville himself: —

"It cannot be denied," says he, "that many reasons authorise us to treat you as an enemy, but we have no inclination to do so. We know you too well not to be persuaded that your heart has taken no part in the treachery of which you have been the instrument, and we are not so unjust as to punish you for a crime of which we believe you innocent, which you undoubtedly detest as much as we do, and for having been the instrument of which we are satisfied you are now deeply grieved. It is not proper, however, that you should remain here. All will not, perhaps, render you the justice which we accord, and when once our young men shall have sung their war song, they will look upon you only as a traitor, who has delivered over our chiefs to a cruel and ignoble slavery. They will listen only to their own rage, from which we will then be unable to save you." Having said this, they obliged him to leave immediately, and furnished guides to conduct him by a safe route, who did not leave him until he was out of danger.

July 4th the army embarked at daybreak, and crossing the lower end of Lake Ontario coasted the south shore westward. So admirably were the plans of DeNonville arranged and executed that, though aware of the impending blow, the Iroquois knew not in what quarter it would strike, and hence could adopt no general measure of defense. The little barque that had been dispatched to Niagara met the army near Sodus bay July 9th with news of the reinforcements, and then returning westward hovered about the mouth of Irondequoit bay. Iroquois scouts stationed there immediately reported the presence of the vessel, and the Seneca sachems sent warriors to the lake. Posting themselves in the woods at the west end of the sand-bar, near the present location of the Sea Breeze, they were surprised and nearly cut off by Indians of DeNonville's Niagara party who came down the lake shore on foot, the main body being in canoes. This party consisted of one hundred and seventy French *coureurs des bois*, and three hundred western Indians of all nations, enemies of the Iroquois. They arrived at the mouth of Irondequoit July 10th, at the same moment with the army under DeNonville, "by reason of which," remarked Baron La Hontan, "our savage allies, who draw predictions from the merest trifles, foretold, with their usual superstition, that so punctual a meeting infallibly indicated the total destruction of the Iroquois." "The first thing with which I occupied myself on my arrival," writes the French governor, "was to select a post easy to be fortified for securing our bateaux, to the number of two hundred, and as many canoes. July 11th was spent in constructing palisades, fascines and pickets, for securing the dike that separates the lake from the marsh, in which we had placed our bateaux."

On their voyage to Niagara Durantaye's forces had captured and pillaged two parties of English traders, bound to the west under the guidance of a young Canadian named La Fontaine Marion. Baron La Hontan mentions him as an unfortunate young man who became acquainted with the country and savages of Canada by the numerous voyages he made over the continent. After rendering his king good service Marion asked permission of several of the governors-general to continue his travels in further prosecution of his petty traffic, but could never obtain it. As peace existed between the two crowns, he determined to go to New England, where he was well received on account of his enterprise and knowledge of Indian languages. He was engaged to pilot two companies of English through the lakes to the west, and it was those peaceful traders upon whom Durantaye had laid violent hands and brought them captive to Irondequoit. DeNonville had previously sought and received the sanction of the king to treat all Frenchmen found in the service of the English as deserters. While the sixty Englishmen were sent to Montreal and subsequently released, Marion was adjudged a traitor and his doom pronounced. The morning following the arrival of the army at Irondequoit the sentence of death was imposed. On the calm surface of the lake rode the French navy of three small sail. Covering the broad sand-beach were overturned boats and canoes, on the elevated part of the sand-bar stood the half-finished fort of pickets surrounded by the army tents and equipage. "Never," says an eye-witness, "had Canada seen, and never perhaps will it see, a similar spectacle. A camp composed of one-fourth regular troops with the general's suite; one-fourth habitants in four battalions, with the gentry of the country; one-fourth Christian Indians, and finally a crowd of all the barbarous nations, naked, tattooed, and painted over the body with all sorts of figures, wearing horns on their heads, queues down their backs, armed with arrows." For a moment there is a profound hush in camp. All eyes are turned to an open square in the center — a file of soldiers facing the lake and a poor wretch standing alone at the water's edge casting a last despairing glance at the wild scene about him. Then a sharp command is given, a loud report follows, and France has sacrificed another victim to her cruel policy in the form of humble Marion.

The fort, requiring some two thousand palisades in its construction, was completed during the forenoon of July 12th. For its defense and the protection of the boats and stores, DeNonville detached four hundred and forty men under command of D'Orvilliers.[1] At three o'clock in the afternoon the army commenced its march upon the Seneca towns in the interior. The advance guard consisted of three hundred Christian Indians under guidance of an Iroquois afterward known as the grandfather of Brandt, with the western Indians on the left, supported by three companies of *coureurs des bois*, one hundred Ottawas, three hundred Sioux, one hundred Illinois and fifty Hurons. Then

[1] This palisade fortification was built on the sand-bar, at the mouth of Irondequoit bay, about eighty rods from its eastern end. The bar, which is only a narrow sand ridge to the west, is some thirty rods wide at this point, and at the advent of the first white settlers was from fifteen to twenty feet high in places. Several small mounds were scattered over the ground, and many graves were discovered, one marked by a tablet of iron bearing an inscription in some unknown language, which is said to have been neither Spanish, Dutch nor French. During the construction of the Rome, Watertown & Ogdensburg railroad, which crosses the bay on this sand-bar, several button-wood trees, each from twelve to eighteen inches in diameter, were removed. Under some of these were found iron bullets, parts of gun-barrels completely oxidised, iron and stone tomahawks, flint arrow-heads, etc. In 1880 the writer discovered several stone relics and portions of two human skeletons under the roots of a tree then standing on the edge of an excavation near the railroad. The channel connecting the waters of the bay with those of the lake has changed its location three several times within the memory of persons now living; shifting from the extreme eastern end of the bar to the western end, back two-thirds of the distance to the eastern shore of the bay, and finally to its present location in the center of the bar.

followed the regulars and militia, with the rear guard of savages and wood-rangers. Ascending the bluff at the end of the sand-bar and following a well-beaten trail, the army returned to the south among lofty trees sufficiently open to allow the troops to march in three columns. The objective point was Gannagora, and the army made three leagues (nine miles) that afternoon. "We left on the next morning," continues DeNonville in his official report, "with the design of approaching the village as near as we could, to deprive the enemy of the opportunity of rallying and seizing on two very dangerous defiles at two rivers[1] which it was necessary for us to pass and where we should undoubtedly meet them. These two defiles being passed in safety, there still remained a third at the entrance of said village, at which it was our intention to halt. . . . . . . About three o'clock in the afternoon M. de Callières, who was at the head of the three companies commanded by Tonty, De la Durantaye and Du-Lhu, and all our savages fell into an ambuscade of Sonnontouans posted in the vicinity of the defile."

DeNonville gives two accounts of this battle, differing widely, and others are confusing. That of the Abbé de Belmont is the best: —

"The march was a little hurried. The weary troops were dying with thirst. The two bodies found themselves at too great distance from each other. The scouts were deceived; for having come to the barrens, or plains, they found five or six women who were going around in the fields. This was a lure of the Senecas to make them believe that they were all in the village. The territory of Ganesara is very hilly; the village is upon a high hill which is surrounded by three little hills or terraces, at the foot of a valley, and opposite some other hills, between which passes a large brook which in a little valley makes a little marsh, covered with alders. This is the place which they selected for their ambuscade. They divided themselves, posted three hundred men along the falling brook between two hills in a great thicket of beech trees, and five hundred at the bottom of these hills in a marsh among the alders; with the idea that the first ambuscade of three hundred men should let the army pass and then attack them in the rear, which would force it to fall into the second ambuscade, which was concealed at the bottom of the hills in the marsh. They deceived themselves nevertheless, for as the advance guard, which M. de Callières commanded, was very distant from the body under the command of the marquis, they believed it was the entire army. Accordingly as the advance guard passed near the thicket of beeches, after making a terrible whoop (sakaqua!) they fired a volley. The Ottawas and the heathen Indians all fled. The Christian Indians of the mountain and the Sault, and the Abenaquis held fast and gave two volleys. The marquis DeNonville advanced with the main body, composed of the royal troops, to occupy the height of the hill, where there was a little fort of pickets; but the terror and disorder of the surprise were such that there was only M. de Cal-zenne, who distinguished himself there, and M. Dugue, who bringing up the rear guard rallied the battalion of Berthier, which was in flight, and, being at the head of that of Montreal, fired two hundred shots. The marquis, en chemise, sword in hand, drew up the main body in battle order, and beat the drum at a time when scarcely anyone was to be seen. This frightened the three hundred Tsonnontouans of the ambuscade, who

---

[2] Allen and Irondequoit creeks.

fled from above towards the five hundred that were ambushed below. The fear that all the world was upon them made them fly with so much precipitation that they left their blankets in a heap, and nothing more was seen of them."

In his description of the battle Baron La Hontan admits a serious defeat of the French : —

"When we arrived at the foot of the hill on which they lay in ambush, distant about a quarter of a league from the village, they began to utter their ordinary cries, followed with a discharge of musketry. If you had seen, sir, the disorder into which our militia and regulars were thrown among the dense woods, you would agree with me that it would require many thousand Europeans to make head against these barbarians. Our battalions were immediately separated into platoons, which ran without order, pell mell to the right and left, without knowing whither they went. Instead of firing upon the Iroquois, we fired upon each other. It was in vain to call for help from the soldiers of such a battalion, for we could see scarcely thirty paces. In short we were so disordered that the enemy were about to fall upon us club in hand, when our savages, having rallied, repulsed and pursued them so closely, even to their villages, that they killed more than eighty, the heads of which they brought away, not counting the wounded who escaped. We lost on this occasion ten savages and a hundred Frenchmen ; we had twenty or twenty-two wounded, among whom was the good Father Angelran."

Although the savage allies were greatly offended at the refusal of DeNonville to leave his wounded and pursue the fleeing Senecas, the French commander ordered a bivouac on the field. "We witnessed the painful sight of the usual cruelties of the savages," writes the marquis to M. de Seignelay, "who cut the dead into quarters, as is done in slaughter-houses, in order to put them into the kettle; the greater number were opened while still warm, that their blood might be drank. Our rascally Ottawas distinguished themselves particularly by these barbarities and by their poltroonery, for they withdrew from the battle. The Hurons of Michilimaquina did very well, but our Christian Indians surpassed all and performed deeds of valor, especially our Iroquois, on whom we dared not rely having to fight against their own relatives. The Illinois did their duty well. . . . . We learned from some prisoners who had deserted from the Senecas that this action cost them forty-five men killed on the field, twenty-five of whom we had seen at the shambles, the others were seen buried by this deserter ; and over sixty very severely wounded.

The Abbé de Belmont thus continues the narrative : —

"We marched in battle order, waiting for an attack. We descended the hill by a little sloping valley, or gorge, through which ran a brook bordered with thick bushes and which discharges itself at the foot of a hill, in a marsh full of deep mud, but planted with alders so thick that one could scarcely see. There it was that they had stationed their two ambuscades, and where perhaps we would have been defeated, if they had not mistaken our advance guards for the whole army and been so hasty in firing. The marquis acted very prudently in not pursuing them, for it was a trick of the Iroquois, to draw us into a greater ambuscade. The marsh, which is about twenty acres, being passed, we found about three hundred wretched blankets, several miserable guns, and began to perceive the famous Babylon of the Tsonnontouans ; a city or village of bark, situated on the top of a mountain of earth. to which one rises by three terraces or hills. It appeared to us from a distance to be crowned with round towers, but these were only large chests (drums) of bark about four feet in length. set the one in the other about five feet in diameter, in which they keep their Indian corn. The village had been burnt by themselves; it was now eight days since. We found nothing in the town except the cemetery and graves. It was filled with snakes and animals; there was a great mask with teeth and eyes of brass, and a great bear skin with which they disguise in their cabins. There were in the four corners great boxes of grain, which they had not burned. They had outside this post their Indian corn in a piquet fort at the top of a little mountain. Steps were cut down on all sides, where it was knee-high throughout the fort."

On the 15th several old men and women were captured or surrendered, one of the old men being father or uncle of the chief of the Senecas. "After we had obtained from the old man all the information he could impart," continues DeNonville "he was placed in the hands of the reverend Father Bruyas, who, finding that he had some traces of the Christian religion through the instrumentality of the reverend Jesuit fathers. missionaries for twenty years in that village, he set about preparing him for baptism, before turning him over to the Indians who had taken him prisoner. He was baptised. and a little while after they contented themselves at our solicitation. with knocking him on the head with a hatchet instead of burning him according to their custom. Our first achievement this day was to set fire to the fort of which we had spoken. It was eight hundred paces in circumference, well enough flanked for saveges, with a retrenchment advanced for the purpose of communicating with a spring which is half way down the hill, it being the only place where they could obtain water." During the three days following. the French were engaged in the destruction of corn, beans and other produce, multitudes of horses, hogs and various kinds of property belonging to the Senecas; the grain of the small village of St. Michael, or Gannogarae, distant a short league from the large town, being destroyed on the 17th. The Indian allies were busy scouring the country and reported the enemy dispersed through the woods on their retreat to the Cayugas. From this point DeNonville's narration may be quoted directly : —

"On the 19th of July moved our camp in the morning from near the village of St. James or Gannagaro, and encamped before Totiakton.[2] surnamed 'the great village.' or the village of the Conception. distant four leagues from the former. We found there a still greater number of planted fields, and wherewithal to occupy ourselves for many days. . . . . On the 21st went to the small village of Gannounata,[3] distant two leagues from the larger, where all the old and new corn was destroyed the same day, though the quantity was as large as in the other villages. It was at the gate of

---

1 Boughton hill.

2 It was at this village that the *procès verbal* (act of taking formal possession of the country) was read.

3 This place the fourth Seneca village, is supposed to have been about two miles southeast of East Avon, at the source of a small stream which empties into the Conesus, near Avon springs. It was called Dyu-do-o-sot, by the Senecas, from its location "at the spring."

this village that we found the arms of England, which Sieur Dongan, governor of New York, had caused to be placed there contrary to all right and reason, in the year 1684, having antedated the arms as of the year 1683, although it is beyond question that we first discovered and took possession of that country, and for twenty consecutive years have had Fathers Frémin, Garnier, etc., as stationary missionaries in all these villages. On the 22d we returned to Totiakton, to continue there the devastation already commenced. On the 23d we sent a large detachment of almost the entire army . . . . . to complete the destruction of all the corn still standing in the distant woods. About seven o'clock in the morning seven Illinois, coming alone from their country to war against the Iroquois, arrived at the camp as naked as worms, bow in hand, to the great joy of those whom Sieur de Tonty had brought to us. About noon of the same day we finished the destruction of the Indian corn. We had the curiosity to estimate the whole quantity, green as well as ripe, which we had destroyed in the four Seneca villages, and found that it would amount to 350,000 minots of green, and 50,000 of old corn [1,200,000 bushels]. We can infer from this the multitude of people in these four villages, and the great suffering they will experience from this devastation.

"Having nothing more to effect in that country, we left our camp in the afternoon of the same day to rejoin our bateaux. We advanced only two leagues. On our way a Huron surprised a Seneca who appeared to be watching our movements. He was killed on the spot because he refused to follow us. On the 24th of July we reached our bateaux after marching six leagues. We halted there on the next day, the 25th, in order to make arrangements for leaving on the 26th, after having destroyed the redoubt we had built. We dispatched the barque for Cataracouy, which we had found with the other two at Ganniatarontagouat, to advise the intendant of the result of our expedition, and by that opportunity sent back those of our camp who were suffering the most from sickness. On the 26th we set out for Niagara, resolved to occupy that post as a retreat for all our Indian allies, and thus afford them the means of continuing, in small detachments, the war against the enemy whom they have not been able to harass hitherto, being too distant from them and having no place to retire to."

CHAPTER IX.

Totiakton — Its Ancient and Modern History — DeNonville's Return Route to the Sand-Bar.

THE history of Totiakton is a matter of local interest, and the positive identification of its former site will explain to many inquiring minds the "mystery" regarding the numberless antiquities discovered in its neighborhood. In 1677 Wentworth Greenhalgh made a journey from Albany to the Indians westward, lasting from May 27th to July 14th. In his *Observations* (*Col. Mss.*, *III.*, p. 252) Mr. Greenhalgh says: —

"Tiotehatton lyes on the brinke or edge of a hill, has not much cleared ground, is neare the river Tiotehatton, which signifies 'bending;' itt lyes to westward of Canagorah about thirty miles, contains about one hundred and twenty houses, being ye largest of

all ye houses wee saw, ye ordinary being about fifty or sixty feet and some one hundred
and thirty or one hundred and forty foott long, with thirteen or fourteen fires in one
house, they have a good store of corne growing about a mile to ye northward of the
towne. Being att this place the 17th of June, there came fifty prisoners from the south-
west-ward, they were of two nations some whereof have few gunns, ye other none at
all; one nation is about ten days journey from any Christians and trade only with one
greatt house nott farre from ye sea, and ye other trade only, as they say, with a black
people; this day of them was burnt two women and a man, and a child killed with a
stone, att night we heard a greatt noyse, as if ye houses had all fallen, butt itt was only ye

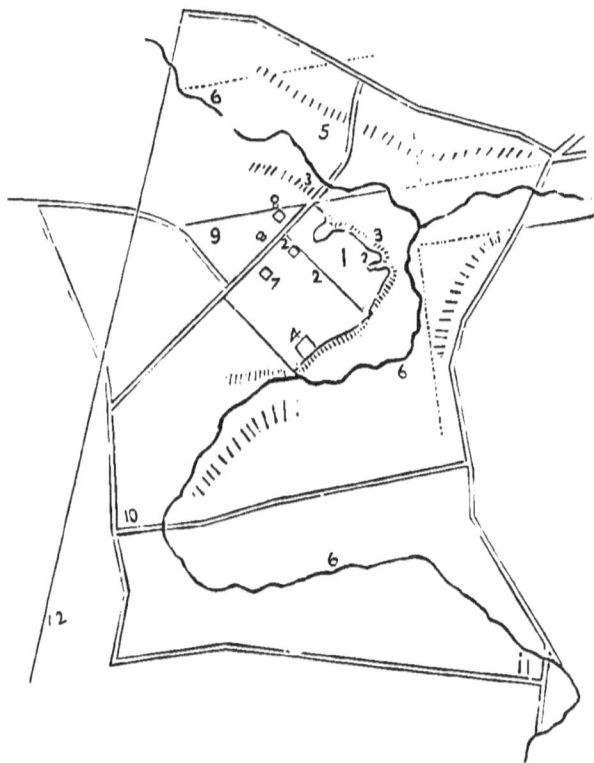

1 Totiakton. 2, 2, 2 Cemeteries. 3, 3. 3 Bluffs. 4 Palisaded Fort. 5 Spring. 6, 6, 6 Honeoye Outlet. 7 J. T
Sheldon. 8 J. Russell. 9 Sheldon's Plain. 10 Sibleyville. 11 Honeoye Falls. 12 Line between Mindon and East Rush.

MAP OF TOTIAKTON AND VICINITY.

inabitants driving away ye ghosts of ye murthered. The 18th, goeing to Canagorah,
wee overtook ye prisoners; when ye soldiers saw us they stopped each his prisoner and
made him sing, and cutt off their fingers, and slasht their bodys with a knife, and when
they had sung each man confessed how many men in his time he had killed."

Totiakton was distant from Gannagora just eleven miles in a northwest direction. Its former site was located by O. H. Marshall in 1847. Blacksmith, the aged Seneca chief from whom Mr. Marshall obtained much information, called this village De-yu-di-haak-doh, which he said signifies "the bend," from its location on a bend of the creek. In this he agrees with Greenhalgh. The present writer has searched out the old town site and prepared the foregoing map of the locality from personal survey.

It is in the town of Mendon, Monroe county, on the northeasternmost bend of Honeoye outlet, two miles north of Honeoye Falls, and exactly twelve and one-half miles in an air line due south of the center of Rochester. In this vicinity the Honeoye flows in a beautiful valley varying from one-fourth to three-fourths of a mile in width, and the channel twists and turns in all directions through the fertile bottom. The ancient town was located on the table land which projects into the west side of the valley in the form of a bold bluff, facing the east, at an elevation of about one hundred and fifty feet above the water. This ground was purchased by Abner Sheldon, in 1802, and is now included in the estate of his son J. F. Sheldon, a gentleman whose courtesy and valuable assistance in the collection of many facts connected with this subject will be long and gratefully remembered. The so-called "clear ground," when Abner Sheldon came in possession, consisted of "oak openings," and a number of large trees were then scattered about the old town site. Judging from the limits within which relics have been found, the Indian village occupied an area of about twenty-five acres. A plentiful supply of water was obtained from springs situated along the base of the bluff to the north. A fine "medicine" spring of sulphur-water is now in operation. The ground has been under cultivation seventy-five years, yielding an annual harvest of antiquities including human bones, gun-barrels, locks, knives and hatchets of iron; tomahawks, arrow-heads, pestles, skinners, etc., of stone; wampum and beads of clay; pottery, brass kettles and trinkets, brass rings bearing the legend I. H. S., pipes, bullets, etc., etc. Three cemeteries have been discovered in locations designated on the map, and all skeletons unearthed have been found in a sitting posture, facing the east.

On the edge of the bluff, about eighty-five rods southeast of, and overlooking the old town, Mr. Sheldon discovered the ruins of a palisade inclosure, occupying half an acre of land. It was nearly square in form and built of logs twelve feet long set closely together in the earth to the depth of four feet. At the date of its discovery the timber was greatly decayed, many of the palisades having rotted to the ground. It was doubtless erected by the Indians who rallied immediately after DeNonville's departure, as a temporary abode and defense prior to their permanent settlement elsewhere. The statement of De-Nonville and other historians of the expedition, regarding the immense amount of corn destroyed by the French troops, has been questioned by late writers, yet a thorough survey of old Totiakton and its environs cannot fail to impress one with a sense of the good judgment exercised by the aboriginal inhabitants in its selection as a place of permanent abode, and the superior advantages possessed by the natives for the cultivation of the soil. About two hundred acres of ground lying southwest of the old Indian village presents a surprisingly smooth, level surface, and was long known as "Abraham's plain." It is now termed "Sheldon's plain." The Indian corn fields mentioned by Greenhalgh were in the oak openings on this plain, and the rich flats in the valley bottom were undoubtedly cultivated to some extent.

DeNonville states that the French left Totiakton in the afternoon of July 23d, and advanced two leagues (six miles). On the following day they reached their bateaux at the mouth of Irondequoit bay, after marching six leagues or eighteen miles. It is evident that the expedition did not return to Irondequoit over the same route by which it reached Totiakton, and the course pursued by the army on its return to the sand-bar has never, within the knowledge of the present writer, been described or suggested in print. As early as 1682 the French had become accustomed to all the woods and acquainted with all the roads through them (*Col. Mss.*, *IX.*, 195), and the Jesuits, several of whom accompanied the expedition, had occupied missions in all the Seneca towns for a period of twenty years, and doubtless understood every mile of Indian path east of the Genesee. So well known and public a thoroughfare as the portage trail between Red creek ford and Irondequoit landing could not have escaped their knowledge. Personal researches have satisfied the writer that the Indians once had a road from the Honeoye outlet to Red creek ford. This trail crossed the Honeoye north of old Totiakton, ran nearly west to an Indian village at the present East Rush cemetery, and thence northwest to the farm now owned by Marvin Williams half a mile south of West Henrietta corners, where evidences of early Indian occupation have been frequently found. A second trail left the Honeoye above Rush junction, ran north *via* Hart's Corners and crossed the farm of David Ely in its course straight to the town on the Williams farm, which is about six miles from old Totiakton. This place would have been DeNonville's camping ground on the night of July 23d if he had followed this trail. At the east base of the hill upon which the town was located is a large pond said to have been the original source of Red creek. The distance from the camp down the Red creek trail to the ford, and *via* the portage trail and Irondequoit landing to the sand-bar, is about twenty-two miles. If the French army pursued this route it passed over the present site of Rochester; but it would appear that this road is much too long.

The writer has traced a trail from the Irondequoit landing-path at the residence of Charles M. Barnes in Brighton, across the Pittsford road to an old town site on Allen's creek in the town of Pittsford, which ran up the east side of the creek directly south. If this trail continued on the same general course it would strike Totiakton. On this line, a short distance north of Mendon Center, are several large ponds fed by springs, where the Senecas went to fish, and numerous indications of Indian camps have been found the entire length of the Allen's creek valley. The distance from the old Indian settlement, by the present road, to the mouth of Irondequoit bay is about twenty-two miles, and this agrees more perfectly with DeNonville's estimate of eight leagues, or twenty-four miles. That an Indian path once extended over this line from Irondequoit to Mendon can hardly be doubted, though its exact course is not known, and it is very probable that the French army returned to the sand-bar on this trail.

CHAPTER X.

Strength of the Iroquois — A Terrible Revenge — French Invasions — Irondequoit a Place of Great Importance in Colonial Times — Fort des Sables — Charlevoix Describes the Casconchiagon — Captain Schuyler Builds a Trading-House at Irondequoit Landing — His Official Instructions — Oliver Culver Discovers the Ruins of the Trading-House — Senecas Sell the Lower Genesee Country to the King of England — British Armies at Irondequoit.

THE early French ignored the native names of people and places in many instances, and applied such designations as pleased themselves. Occasionally Indian names were used, but not as a rule. The Mohawk canton was called Anniegue, the Oneida Onneiout, the Onondaga Onnontague, Cayuga Oioguen, and the Seneca Sonnontouân. In 1665 the Jesuits estimated the number of warriors at 2,340. In 1667 Colonel Courcey, agent for Virginia, stated that the Five Nations had 2,150 warriors. Wentworth Greenhalgh in 1677 placed the number of fighting men at 2,150. In 1685 DeNonville gave the numerical strength of the Iroquois as follows: Mohawks 250, Oneidas 150, Onondagas 300, Cayugas 200, Senecas 1,200, or 2,100 men all told, capable of bearing arms. Marshall estimates the entire population about that date as 7,000, but Bancroft says that in 1660 the whole number could not have varied much from ten thousand; and their warriors strolled as conquerors from Hudson's bay to Carolina, and from the Kennebec to the Tennessee. The Seneca was the most powerful nation of the league, and had all its braves been at home when the French arrived at Irondequoit, the history of DeNonville's expedition w‑‑‑' ' [...] ibtless record a disastrous repulse of the invaders, who [...] ted and put to flight eight hundred Senecas. The latter [...] part of their warriors were absent, fighting distant foes, [...] the engagement with the French consisted of only four [...] The Seneca loss probably did not greatly exceed one [...] these were old men and boys not reckoned active war‑ [...] strength was but slightly diminished. They retreated to Canandaigua, and in an incredibly short space of time collected a force of one thousand men, who took the trail for Niagara. Upon the completion of the fort at that place by the French, a detachment under La Hontan was ordered west to relieve the garrison of Fort St. Joseph at Detroit. That officer portaged the falls of Niagara and embarked his troops at Schlosser. The party had barely left the land when the thousand Iroquois appeared on the shore in close pursuit. The French succeeded in reaching Lake Erie in safety, and, distancing the heavy canoes of the Indians, escaped to the north shore.

In 1688 DeNonville induced the Five Nations to send a delegation to Montreal for the purpose of agreeing upon terms of peace. The Iroquois dispatched seventeen hundred men to the St. Lawrence, five hundred visiting Montreal as a peace delegation, and twelve hundred awaiting the result near at hand. A treaty was concluded, but one Kondiaronk, a Huron chief, determined to frustrate it. When a party of the Iroquois peace envoys were returning up the St. Lawrence, Kondiaronk attacked them, killed several and captured the rest. He represented that he was acting upon an understanding with the French, and, when informed that he had destroyed a peace delegation, affected great indignation, released his prisoners and advised them to avenge their fallen friends. During the summer twelve hundred Iroquois landed on the south side of Montreal, and destroyed the place, slaughtering men, women and children without mercy. Smith says that "a thousand French were slain in the invasion, and twenty-six carried into captivity and burned alive. Many more were made prisoners in another attack in October, and the lower part of the Island of Montreal wholly destroyed."

War between France and England occurred soon after, lasting until 1697. With few exceptions the Iroquois remained implacable enemies of the French, and the latter made several invasions of the Iroquois country. In 1689 La Hontan entered New York from the south shore of Lake Erie with an army of western Indians, and had several engagements with the Iroquois, but his battle grounds have never been identified. In February, 1692, an army of French and Huron allies attacked the hunting parties of the Senecas in Upper Canada. In 1693 the Mohawk country was devastated. The last French expedition against the Five Nations of which we have any record occurred in 1696, when Count de Frontenac landed an army at Oswego and destroyed the crops of the Onondagas and Oneidas. That expeditions were made to the Seneca country, and battles fought here of which no known record exists, is fully believed by those who have given the subject of Indian antiquities thought and study. Did space permit, many excellent reasons influencing this belief might be presented. The French occupancy of Western New York has never been fully recorded, and lasting memorials of unknown struggles upon our home soil have, for years, proved perplexing obstacles to the completion of a perfect history. From 1689 to the treaty of Utrecht, in 1713, the French and English ma said to have been continually at war in all our great lake region, and the contest for dominion and control of the Indian trade ceased only upon the final overthrow of French power in Canada. During all this period Oswego, Irondequoit and Niagara remained subjects of contention.

In April, 1700, Robert Livingstone, then secretary of Indian affairs for New York, made a journey to Onondaga to ascertain the condition of matters within his jurisdiction. In his report of the trip to the earl of Bellomont, he says: "I do humbly offer that it is morally impossible to secure the Five Nations to the English interest any longer, without building forts and securing the passes that lead to their castles." Mr. Livingstone recommended the erection of a fort between Lakes Erie and Huron at a point 744 miles southwest of Albany, and mentions the route to that place as follows: "Albany to Terindequat [Irondequoit] at the Lake of Cadaracqui [Ontario] 400 miles, thence to Onyagara where the great fall is eighty miles, from thence to the beginning of Swege [Erie] lake 64 miles, to Swege creek and from thence to Wawachtonok 160 miles." He also recommended a fort on the Onondaga river, to be garrisoned with 100 youths, and remarked: "It is true that the French do trade, and have small hutts and berks which they call forts at some of those Indian habitations where they have priests."

The governor of Canada also desired to erect forts, one at Niagara, "the second at Jerondaquat, that is, on this side of Cadaracqui lake where the path goes up to the Sinnekes castles, about thirty miles from where the Sinnekes have now their castles." August 20th, 1701, Lieutenant-Governor Nanfan reported to the lords of trade that he had procured from the Five Nations an instrument whereby they conveyed to the crown of England a tract of land 800 miles long and 400 broad, including all their beaver hunting, which tract began at Jarondigat." [1]

In 1716, the French erected a building near the present site of the Sea Breeze hotel at the northwest angle of Irondequoit bay and Lake Ontario.[2] It was known to the French as Fort des Sables, and appears to have been considered quite an important station. At a private conference held in June, 1717, between Governor Hunter of New York and two sachems of each of the Five Nations, the latter said: —

"We have had two messages from hence — one last fall and another this winter — to inquire if the French had built a fort and planted a garrison on this side the great lake, at a place called Terondoquat, belonging to the Sinnekes; we could not give them a positive answer till we had sent as far as the Senekes; but now can tell your excellency that there is no such thing, but that the French have built a trading-house at the said place, where they supply our Indians with powder and lead to fight against the Flatheads and other enemies of the Five Nations; and we must likewise acquaint you that

[1] *Col. Mss., IV.*, 888.
[2] For the identification of this location I am indebted to my good friend B. Fernow, keeper of historical documents of the state library at Albany.

our people are furnished with other goods also at the said French trading-house, as clothing and other necessaries, which stops a great deal of peltry coming hither; but the French are supplied with all those goods from the people here at Albany, which goes first to Canada and from thence up Mount Royal river and so on to Terondoquat, where the French trading-house is built upon ground belonging to the Sennekes. If you will stop that trade of goods being carried from hence to Canada the other trade will fall of course."

In May, 1720, Lawrence Clawson was sent to Niagara to protest against the erection of forts on the Seneca lands, by the French, and in his journal says: "On the 7th I returned to Tjerondequatt, where I mett a French smith sent by the governor of Canada to work for the Sinnekies gratis."

It would seem that Fort des Sables was not in the ordinary sense a military post. Charlevoix tells us that the French erected cabins, surrounded by pickets, "to which they give beforehand the name of Fort, for they say that in time it will be changed into a real fortress." Rev. John Durant, who passed Irondequoit in 1718, says the French left only one storekeeper and two soldiers at such posts during each winter. In October, 1720, the Sieur de Joncaire left Montreal for Niagara, with two canoes laden with merchandise, and twelve soldiers, "whereof he sent six when he arrived at the fort of Cataraque. He pursued afterward his voyage, but the ice stopped him thirty-five leagues from the mouth of the river of Niagara, where he was obliged to go into another river called Gaschonchiagon, where he passed the winter." Father Charlevoix stopped at Irondequoit bay in May, 1721, on his journey westward, and, writing soon after from Niagara, says: —

"I departed from the river of Sables the 21st, before sunrise; but, the wind continuing against us, we were obliged at ten o'clock to enter the bay of the Tsonnonthouans [Braddock's bay]. Half way from the river of Sables to this bay there is a little river [the Genesee], which I would not have failed to have visited, if I had been sooner informed of its singularity, and of what I have just now learned on my arriving here. They call this river Casconchiagon. It is very narrow and of little depth at its entrance into the lake. A little higher it is one hundred and forty yards wide, and they say it is deep enough for the largest vessels. Two leagues from its mouth we are stopped by a fall which appears to be sixty feet high, and one hundred and forty yards wide. A musket shot higher we find a second of the same width, but not so high by two-thirds. Half a league further a third, one hundred feet high, good measure, and two hundred yards wide. After this we meet with several torrents; and after having sailed fifty leagues further we meet a fourth fall [Portage] every way equal to the third. The course of this river is one hundred leagues, and when we have gone up it about sixty leagues we have but ten to go by land, taking to the right, to arrive at the Ohio, called La Belle Rivière. The place where we meet with it is called Ganos; where an officer worthy of credit (M. de Joncaire) and the same from whom I learnt what I have just now mentioned, assured me that he had seen a fountain the water of which is like oil, and has the taste of iron. He said also that a little further there is another fountain exactly like it, and that the savages make use of its waters to appease all manner of pains. The bay of the Tsonnonthouans is a charming place. A pretty river winds here between two meadows, bordered with little hills, between which we discover

SOUTHEAST VIEW OF THE GREAT CATARACT
ON CASCONCHIAGON OR LITTLE SENECA'S RIVER, LAKE ONTARIO,
1768.

SOUTHEAST VIEW OF THE LOWER CATARACT
ON CASCONCHIAGON [GENESEE] OR LITTLE SENECA'S RIVER, LAKE ONTARIO,
1768.

valleys which extend a great way, and the whole forms the finest prospect in the world, bounded by a great forest of high trees; but the soil appears to be somewhat light and sandy."

The actual occupation of the Seneca country by the French was an incentive to the English to adopt measures for protection of the Indian trade, and in the early summer of 1721 the assembly of New York passed an act for raising the sum of five hundred pounds for securing the Indians to the English interest. This sum Governor Burnet expended chiefly in the establishment of a settlement at Irondequoit. His project met with the hearty approval of the authorities at Albany, and a small company of volunteers was promptly organised to carry it into effect. This company consisted of Captain Peter Schuyler, jr., Lieutenant Jacob Verplanck, Gilleyn Verplanck, Johannis Van den Bergh, Peter Gronendyck, David Van der Heyden and two others whose names are unknown. Governor Burnet's instructions to Captain Schuyler were as follows:—

"You are with all expedition to go with this company of young men that are willing to settle in the Sinnekes' country for a twelvemonth to drive a trade with the far Indians that come from the upper lakes, and endeavor by all suitable means to persuade them to come and trade at Albany or with this new settlement. You are not to trade with the four hithermost nations but to carry your goods as farr as the Sinnekes' country to trade with them or any other Indian nations that come hither. You are to make a settlement or trading house either at Jerondoquat or any other convenient place on this side of Cadarachqui lake upon the land belonging to the Sinnekes, and use all lawfull means to draw the furr trade thither by sending notice to the farr Indians that you are settled there for their ease and incouragement by my order, and that they may be assured they shal have goods cheaper here than ever the French can afford them at Canada, for the French must have the principal Indian goods from England, not having them of their own. You are also to acquaint all the far Indians that I have an absolute promise and engagement from the Five Nations that will not only suffer them to pass freely and peaceably through their country, but will give them all due encouragement and sweep and keep the path open and clean when ever they intend to come and trade with this province. Being informed that there are sundry French men called by the Dutch 'bush loopers,' and by the French *coureurs du bois*, who have for several years abandoned the French colony of Canada and live wholly among the Indians, if any such come to trade with you, with their furrs, you may supply them and give them all possible incouragement to come hither where they shall be supplyed with Indian goods much cheaper than at Canada. Altho the place where you settle be land belonging to the crown of Great Britain, both by the surrender of the natives and the treaty of peace with France, nevertheless you are to send out skouts and spyes and be upon your guard, the French not being to be trusted, who will use all means to prevent the far Indians coming to trade with you or their coming to Albany. You are to keep an exact dyary or journall of all your proceedings of any consequence, and keep a constant correspondence with the commissioners of the Indian affairs at Albany, whom I will order to give me an account thereof from time to time, and whenever you shall receive orders from me to treat with the Sinnekes, or any of the Five Nations, you are to be carefull to minute down your proceedings and their answers, and to send them to me with the first opportunity, inclosing them to the commissioners of the Indian affairs who will forward them with all expedition, and if any matters of great moment and fit to be kept very secret do occur, you are to send an account thereof to me in a letter sealed, which may be inclosed to the commissioners in order to be forwarded, and you are not obliged to mention such matters in your letter to the commissioners. When you come to the Sinnekes' country you are to give them a belt of wampum in token that they are to give credit to you as my agent to treat with them of all matters relating to the public service and the benefit of the trade, and at your desire to furnish you with a number of their people as you shall want for your assistance and safety on such conditions as you and they can agree upon. When you have pitched upon a convenient place for a trading-house, you are to endeavor to purchase a tract of land in the king's name, and to agree with the Sinnekes for it which shall be paid by the publick in order that it may be granted by patent to those that shall be the first settlers there for their incouragement. You are not to hinder or molest any other British subjects who are willing to trade there on their own hazard and account for any Indian goods, rum only excepted. You are to communicate to the company such articles of your instructions as shall be proper for their regulation from time to time. If you judge it necessary you may send one or two of your company either among the far Indians, or to come to Albany, as the necessary service of the company shall require, but not above two of the said company, of which yourself may be one, will be permitted to be absent at one time. When you are about to absent yourself from the said settlement you are to leave a copy of such part of instructions with the lieutenant as you judge necessary for his regulation. All the goods and merchandize that you and said company shall take away with you are to be upon one joint stock and account and all your profit and losse to be the same. Given under my hand at the manor of Livingston the eleventh day of September in the eighth year of his majesty's reign, anno Dom. 1721.

"WM. BURNET."

Additional Instructions.

"Whereas it is thought of great use to the British interest to have a settlement upon the nearest port of the Lake Eree near the falls of Iagara, you are to endeavor to purchase in his majesty's name of the Sinnekes or other native propriators all such lands above the falls of Iagara fifty miles to the southward of the said falls which they can dispose off, you are to have a copy of my propositions to the Five Nations and their answer, and to use your utmost endeavors that they do perform all that they have promised therein, and that none of these instructions be shewn to any person or persons but what you shall think necessary to communicate to the lieutenant and the rest of the company."

Upon his arrival at Irondequoit Captain Schuyler selected a location for his trading-house secure from French surveillance, yet affording easy access from Lake Ontario, and control of all Indian paths leading to the water. The actual site of the building was a little plateau overlooking the noted Indian landing on Irondequoit creek, at the eastern terminus of the grand portage trail. This spot may be regarded as the most important point in all the lower Genesee country. It was the great Indian landing-place from Lake Ontario, and general trading-ground of the early tribes. Previous to the building of Fort des Sables the French ran their little sailing vessels up the bay and creek to this landing, and it was doubtless at this place, and not in the Genesee river, that the brigantine of La Salle dropped anchor in June, 1670. There the Senecas went to trade furs for arms, trinkets and brandy; there Father Hennepin left the bartering crew of French and Indians, and wandered deep into the woods, built a chapel of bark wherein, secure from observation and in communion with nature, he performed his religious duties.[1] The house erected by Captain Schuyler's company stood a short distance from the edge of the bluff, with one side facing the creek It was an oblong structure of considerable size. After an occupation lasting one year, Captain Schuyler returned to Albany in September, 1772, with all his company. While excavating the earth for a building upon the same location about 1798, Oliver Culver discovered the foundation logs of a block-house, evidently destroyed by fire, and musket balls, etc., in large quantities. It has been assumed by certain writers that the ruins discovered at the Irondequoit creek landing by Mr. Culver were the remains of a battery or redoubt built by DeNonville, and that his army actually landed at that place, but this is an error. As we have already shown, DeNonville's army landed at the mouth of Irondequoit bay, and the only fortification erected by the French at that time was on the sand-bar. It is supposed, however, that the "first defile" mentioned by DeNonville was the passage through the valley at the Irondequoit landing. The ruins found by Mr. Culver were undoubtedly the lower logs of Captain Schuyler's trading-house.

For many years Irondequoit, as the great pass to the Seneca country, proved a bone of earnest contention between French and English, each nation proposing to build a stone fortress at the entrance of the bay upon obtaining the consent of its rightful owners, the Seneca Indians. In August, 1741, Lieutenant-Governor Clarke, of New York, wrote the lords of trade as follows:—

"I have the honor to inform your lordships that by the means of some people whom I sent last year to reside in the Senecas' country (as usual) I obtained a deed for the lands at Tierrondequat from the sachimes, and I have sent orders to those people to go around the lands in company with some of the sachimes and to mark the trees, that it may be known at all times hereafter how much they have given up to us."

"Deed to His Majesty of the Lands Around Tierondequat.

"To all people to whome these presents shall or may come We, Tenekokaiwee, Tewasajes and Staghreche, Principall Sachims of the Sinnekes' country, native Indians of the province of New York, send greeting. Know yee that for sundry good causes and considerations us Moveing but More Especially for and in consideration of the value of one hundred pounds currant money of the said province, unto us in hand paid and delivered at and before the ensealing and delivery hereof by the receipt whereof we do hereby acknowledge and therewith to be fully paid and contented thereof and therefrom and of and from every part and parcell thereof, do fully clearly and absolutely request exonerate and discharge them the Said their Executors Administrators and

---

[1] *New Discovery*, p. 109.

Assigns and every of them forever by these presents have therefore given granted released and forever quit Claimed and by these presents for us and our defendants do give grant release and forever quit claim unto our most gracious Sovereign Lord George the second by the grace of God of Great Britain France and Ireland King Defender of the faith etc., his heirs and Successors all our Right title and Interest Claime property profession and demand of in and to all that tract of land Scituate lying and being in the county of Albany beginning on the bank of the Oswego lake six miles easterd of Tierondequat and runs from thence along the Lake westward twenty miles and from the Lake southeastward thirty miles keeping that distance from the Lake all the way from the beginning to the end with all and Singular of woods underwoods trees mines mineralls quarrys hereditaments and appertenances whatsoever and the Reversion and Reversions Remainder and Remainders Rents Issues and Profitts thereof to have and to hold all and singular the above bargained premisses with the appurtenances unto our said most gracious Sovereign Lord his heirs Successors and Assigns to the sole and only proper use benefitt and behoof of our said Sovereign Lord his heirs Successors and Assigns for ever, in Testimony whereof we have hereinto sett our marks and seals this tenth day of January in the fourteenth year of his Majesties Reign annoq: Dom: 174?.

DEKOSCHTEN
alias TENEHOKAIWEE.   Sergrmen.

Signed Sealed and Delivered
In the presence of   TWESSA   Sergrmen.

HENDRYCK WEMPEL
JACOBUS VAN EPS   STAICHRESEH   Sergrmen.
PHILIP RYDER

" Albany 3d October 1741 appeared before Philip Livingston Esquire one of his Majesties Councill for the Province of New York Hendrik Wemp Jacobus Van Eps and Philip Ryder who declared on the holy Evangelists of Almighty God that they saw the within named Tenehokaiwe Tewassajes and Staghreche Sachims Sign Scale and deliver ye within deed as their voluntary act and deed for the use therein mentioned.

"P: LIVINGSTON."

Governor Clarke made repeated efforts to effect the settlement of an English colony at Irondequoit, without success. Oswego, being on the main water communication between Albany and Lake Ontario, and Niagara, controlling the passage to Erie and the western lakes, became the principal points of contest, and great forts were built at those places while Irondequoit remained a simple trading station. July 1st, 1759, General Prideaux, with Sir William Johnson second in command, left Oswego with an army of two thousand men and five hundred Indians on an expedition against Fort Niagara, at the mouth of Niagara river, then occupied by the French. The expedition was supplied with heavy artillery and all necessary military equipments for a protracted siege, and was transported in vessels, bateaux and canoes. Coasting the south shore of Lake Ontario, the first night's encampment was at Sodus, the second at Irondequoit and the third in Braddock's bay — which latter place was then named Prideaux bay, in honor of the English commander, who was killed a few days later during the siege.   At each halting-place discharges of artillery were made to inspire their Indian allies with courage, and their foes with terror. Upon the surrender of Fort Niagara Sir William Johnson, with nearly all his army and six hundred prisoners, returned down the lake to Oswego, again camping at Irondequoit.   In 1764 General Bradstreet left Oswego upon an expedition against the hostile western tribes under Pontiac.   During the passage up Lake Ontario his army, consisting of twelve hundred troops, followed by Sir William Johnson with six hundred Indians, also encamped at Irondequoit. Israel Putnam, of Bunker Hill fame, was then lieutenant-colonel of the Connecticut battalion in the expedition, and several other men who subsequently became illustrious patriots of the Revolution, were officers of Bradstreet's army.

CHAPTER XI.

The Seneca Castles on the Genesee — Treaty of Peace with the English — Decline of Iroquois Power — Sullivan's Campaign against the Senecas — Fate of Lieutenant Boyd — Sullivan's Troops on the Site of Rochester.

THE red men seldom rebuilt upon the site of a town destroyed by enemies, though they occasionally settled in the near vicinity of such places.   As a rule the surviving inhabitants removed to a distance.   After the destruction of their four principal villages by DeNonville, the Senecas sought other localities for their settlements.   Towns sprang up in the lower Genesee country, mainly on the trails leading to Irondequoit bay, but as early as 1715 their castles were located on the middle and upper Genesee.   The frequent removals and establishment of new towns render any chronological account of the Seneca settlements impossible.   The soil of the Genesee valley is rich with humble memorials of their presence in every part of its rugged uplands and alluvial flats, and, did space permit, it might prove an interesting theme to point out existing evidences of several large Indian towns which were located in the immediate neighborhood of Rochester; but this shall be our task at some future day; at present we must hasten with the record of changes contemporary with the close of aboriginal occupation.   For a period of twenty years following the termination of French dominion in Western New York in 1759 there are few events of direct local bearing recorded in history.   The Iroquois had steadily maintained their sole right to possession of the Genesee country against all comers, and upon the overthrow of the French at Niagara naturally sided with them against the conquerors, entering into active preparations to rid the country of every Englishman. Immediately succeeding the treaty of Paris in 1763 and consequent end of the French war, the Iroquois decided to acquiesce in the general submission to British rule. April 3d, 1764, a preliminary treaty was arranged between the Senecas and English at Johnson Hall, and ratified at Niagara the following summer under a peremptory threat of General Brad-street to at once destroy the Seneca settlements if the peace compact was not promptly and fully confirmed by all the nation. This treaty was the beginning of the end of Indian domination in the Genesee country. Among other con-cessions wrung from the Senecas by the terms of this peace was the surrender of title to lands along the Niagara river between Lakes Ontario and Erie. Having large military forces at Oswego and Niagara, the English were prepared to follow up this acquisition of title by actual occupation and control of the grounds ceded, and the foothold thus obtained by the whites was never relin-quished.

The diversion of the direct channel of western trade to and through Oswego eastward, upon the ascendency of the English, rendered Irondequoit and the lower Genesee comparatively unimportant stations, or ports of the Senecas. Individual traders and small parties of whites often visited the Indian settle-ments and British troops occasionally passed through the dark forests, but the border line of civilisation was far to the eastward, and the exciting events pre-ceding the struggle between the colonists and mother-land failed to disturb the primitive peace of our home wilderness. Through all the dreadful scenes of the Revolution the occurrences on the lower Genesee were confined to the pas-sage of war parties of British and Indians, but the great "vale of the Senecas" became a stronghold and secure retreat for predatory bands of tories and sav-ages, who made frequent, desolating incursions and "hung like a scythe of death" about all the border towns of the American colonists. In retaliation Gen-eral John Sullivan invaded the Genesee country with an army of four thousand men during the summer of 1779, and destroyed the Indian settlements. On his march up the Tioga — or Chemung, as it is now called — he attacked and routed some twelve or fifteen hundred British troops, tories and savages under Butler, Johnson and Brandt, who were intrenched at Newtown, about four miles below the present city of Elmira. The retreating enemy were followed to Geneva, Canandaigua and Conesus. Sullivan expected to find the famous Genesee Indian castle at the mouth of the Canaseraga creek, but in all his army there was not a single person sufficiently acquainted with the country to guide a party outside the Indian trails, and on his arrival at Ka-naugh-saws (head of Conesus lake) he dispatched Lieutenant Thomas Boyd of Morgan's rifle corps, with twenty-six men, to ascertain the location of the town. Boyd's little band crossed the Conesus outlet and followed the trail to a village on the Canaseraga, about seven miles distant, which was found deserted, the fires still burning.

The party encamped near the town and on the following morning, September 13th, 1779, started to rejoin the army. Just as they were descending the hill at the base of which the army lay, five or six hundred warriors and loyalists under Brandt and Butler rose up before them and with horrid yells closed in upon the little band from every side. In the terrific struggle that followed, all the party were killed except Murphy, McDonald, Putnam and a Canadian, who escaped, and Boyd and Parker, who were captured. The prisoners were conducted to Little Beard's Town (now Cuylerville), which was then termed the Chinesee castle, and upon their refusal to impart information regarding Sullivan's army were turned over to the Indians. Parker was simply beheaded, but Boyd was subjected to the most horrible tortures that savage ingenuity could inflict. Sullivan's soldiers, who had crossed the Genesee to attack Little Beard's Town, were so close at the time that the advance found the remains of Boyd and Parker while the blood was still oozing from the headless trunks. They were buried that evening with military honors, under a clump of wild plum trees, at the junction of two small streams which form Beard's creek, and a large mound was raised over the grave.[1]

Previous to the arrival of Sullivan's army the Indians had sent all their women and children to Silver lake, and upon the first appearance of the American troops on the west side of the river the enemy fled precipitately. Brandt with his warriors and the British regulars took the Moscow trail for Buffalo creek and Niagara, while the tory rangers went to the Caledonia springs. From that place Walker, the noted British spy, was sent to Fort Niagara with instructions to obtain a sufficient number of boats to transport the tories and meet them at the mouth of the Genesee river. The rangers then came down the trail to Red creek ford at the rapids in South Rochester (see chapter VI.), where they divided into two parties, one going directly to the lake, by the St. Paul street route; the other over the portage trail to Irondequoit landing and the tories' retreat in the great ox-bow curve of the Irondequoit creek, thence across the country to the mouth of the Genesee, where the boats from Niagara found the entire party in a starving condition some days later. Little Beard's Town is said to have been the extreme western point reached by Sullivan, and it has long been a question of considerable interest whether any part of his army descended the Genesee to the vicinity of Rochester. Following the arrival of the troops at the Genesee castle all property of the Indians was ruthlessly destroyed, including one hundred houses, some two hundred acres of grain, large crops of beans and potatoes, and several orchards, one of which contained fifteen hundred trees. "While this work was in progress at Little Beard's Town," says Norton, "General Sullivan, according to the undisputed tradition of years, sent Generals Poor and Maxwell down the river to Cannawaugus, which place they destroyed, and on this return march likewise burned Big Tree village. Gen-

[1] For an account of the final disposition of their bones, the reader is referred to chapter XIX. of this history.

eral Sullivan makes no mention of this fact, nor is the destruction of Canna-waugus recorded in the numerous journals kept by officers of Sullivan's army ; the conclusion is irresistible that no portion of the army got as far north as Cannawaugus, and that that village escaped the general destruction ; Big Tree village, it is sufficient to say, had no existence on the Genesee until after the Revolution." [1]

While the return route of Sullivan's army is fully understood, it is not prob-able that the minor incidents of each scouting expedition were considered of sufficient importance to merit special record. Sullivan's spies undoubtedly followed the retreating enemy some distance, and one or more parties of scouts may have trailed the tories to Irondequoit and the mouth of the river. The rangers certainly believed that Sullivan's men were in their immediate vicinity, as they concealed themselves in the brush and dared not shoot a gun, build a fire or expose their precious carcasses until the appearance of Walker with the boats for their removal. The Indians retreated to Fort Niagara, and most of the Senecas remained there during the winter, which was unusually severe. The food furnished by the British being insufficient and of inferior quality, hun-dreds of Indians died from starvation and scurvy. Few ever returned to their old homes east of the Genesee, the main body of Senecas settling at Buffalo creek, Squawkie hill, Little Beard's Town and Cannawaugus. Some came upon the lower Genesee, and as late as 1796 the town located on the Culver farm in Irondequoit (see chapter VI.) numbered over three hundred inhabitants. Their power as a nation was completely broken, and upon the conclusion of peace between the United States and England, the latter nation made no provision for her defeated Indian allies, leaving them entirely to the mercy of the Americans.

---

[1] *Sullivan's Campaign*, by A. Tiffany Norton, p. 166. While this statement of Norton's would appear to effectually dispose of the question, it is quite certain that the pioneers of the lower Genesee firmly believed that Sullivan's army, or some considerable portion of the troops, actually came within the present boundaries of Rochester. In 1810 Jacob Miller settled the Red creek ford farm on the east bank of the Genesee, and found a number of decaying boats near the mouth of Red creek. Mr. Miller was repeatedly informed by Indians that these were the remains of boats used by Sullivan's soldiers who came down the river in pursuit of the tory rangers.

About 1821 Charles M. Barnes, Calvin and Russell Eaton and a fourth boy named Stanley were at play on the bank of Allen's creek in Brighton, near the crossing of East avenue. They noticed a man, apparently about seventy years of age, looking around at various objects, and inquired what he was searching for. The stranger replied "I was in Sullivan's army, and the first night after the fight I slept under a large white oak tree that stood near this spot. The place has altered very much, but I recollect that it was under a tree that stood close to the creek." The boys pointed out a large white oak stump standing on the east bank of the stream some rods below, and the stranger thought that might have been the exact spot where he slept, but could not say positively, as the surroundings were so changed. He told the boys his name and rank and related several incidents of Sullivan's march. Mr. Barnes is still living, hale and hearty at seventy-three, and has a distinct remembrance of the cir-cumstance, though the name of the stranger was forgotten years ago. The relation of similar incidents was common among our early settlers, and there can be little doubt that they were founded on fact.

CHAPTER XII.

The White Man's Occupancy of the Genesee Country — The Native Title Extinguished — Indian Reservations — Present Indian Population.

THE soldiers of Sullivan's army carried to their eastern homes wonderful tales of Western New York, of its grand forests, natural meadows, rich soil and valuable watercourses, and to many the Genesee country became the land of promise and the Eden of pioneer hopes. At the close of the Revolutionary war all of New York west of German Flats was a wilderness inhabited by Indians only. At the conclusion of peace in 1783 King George III. relinquished his claim to this territory, to the United States. The state of New York asserted her right to all lands extending westerly to Lakes Erie and Ontario, founding her claim mainly as successor to the Five Nations and on the acquiescence of the British crown. Massachusetts resisted this claim upon the ground of prior title to certain portions of the land by virtue of a charter granted to the council of Plymouth by King James I. in 1620. This dispute was settled by a treaty held at Hartford, Connecticut, in December, 1786. Among other conditions of the settlement, Massachusetts relinquished all sovereignty and jurisdiction over all that part of the state of New York lying west of a meridian drawn through Seneca lake, and comprising what were subsequently known as the Phelps & Gorham and Holland Land company's purchases (see *New York Charter*, by O. H. Marshall), reserving the right of preëmption in the soil, or in other words the right to purchase of the Indians. In April, 1788, Oliver Phelps and Nathaniel Gorham purchased of Massachusetts the preëmption right of the territory ceded to that state, comprising some six million acres, for one million dollars. In July of that year these gentlemen extinguished the "native right" to a portion of these lands by purchase of the Indians at a treaty held at Buffalo, and in 1790, being unable to fulfill their agreement with Massachusetts, prevailed on that commonwealth to take back four million acres and reduce the amount of ther purchase money to thirty-one thousand pounds. After settling a portion of their tract, in November, 1790, Phelps and Gorham disposed of nearly all the residue, about 1,264,000 acres, to Robert Morris, who sold the same to Charles Williamson, who held it in trust for Sir William Pulteney. The Pulteney estate was bounded "on the north by Lake Ontario, east by the preëmption line, south by the state of Pennsylvania, west by a transit meridian line due north from latitude 42 to the Genesee river at its junction with the Canaseraga creek, thence by the Genesee river to the south line of Caledonia, thence west twelve miles, and thence northwesterly by the east line of the 'triangle,' twelve miles west of the Genesee river to Lake Ontario." It is not our purpose at this time to trace the succession of title to lands in Western New York. It is sufficient to say that Massachusetts sold the four million acres given up by Phelps and Gorham, to Robert Morris. In 1792–3 Mr. Morris sold nearly all of his interest in lands west of the Genesee river, to Herman Le Roy, William Bayard, Matthew Clarkson, Garrett Boon and John Linklaen, in trust for certain gentlmen in Holland, and this tract was afterward known as the "Holland Purchase." A law permitting aliens to hold real estate was passed soon after, enabling Sir William Pulteney and the Hollanders to assume the titles of their respective estates. By the terms of his transactions with Sir William Pulteney and the Holland company, Mr. Morris was bound to extinguish the whole native title to all lands between Seneca lake and the Niagara frontier, and accordingly a treaty with the Senecas was held at Geneseo (Big Tree) in September, 1797. Of the six million acres in Western New York owned by the Indians previous to Phelps and Gorham's first purchase in 1787, the terms of the Geneseo treaty left for their use only the following described " reservations:"—

" 1. Cannawaugus, two square miles lying on the west bank of the Genesee river, west of Avon. 2 and 3. Big Tree and Little Beard, in all four square miles on the west bank of the Genesee, near Geneseo. 4. Squawkie Hill, two miles square, on the west bank of the Genesee, north of Mount Morris. 5. Gardeau, or Gardow, the "white woman's" reservation, containing about twenty-eight square miles (17.927 acres) on both sides of the Genesee river, between Mount Morris and Portage. 6. Caneadea, sixteen square miles, on both sides of the Genesee above Portage. 7. Oil Spring, one square mile on the line between Alleghany and Cattaraugus counties. 8. Alleghany, forty-four square miles, on both sides of the Alleghany river, near Salamanca. 9. Cattaraugus, forty-two square miles, on both sides and near the mouth of Cattaraugus creek, on Lake Erie, twenty-six miles north of Buffalo. 10. Buffalo, one hundred and thirty square miles, on both sides of Buffalo creek, near Buffalo. 11. Tonawanda, seventy square miles, on both sides of Tonawanda creek, about twenty-five miles from its mouth, and sixteen miles northeast of Buffalo. 12. Tuscarora, one square mile, on the mountain ridge, three miles east of Lewiston."

The Indian title to all these reservations, except Alleghany, Cattaraugus, Tonawanda and Tuscarora, has since been extinguished. As early as 1820 the red man had few representatives in the Genesee valley, and about 1830 they ceased to occupy their old camp grounds along the lower Genesee. In 1826 John De Bay and Samuel Willett, two men who accompanied Clark in his famous western expedition in 1806, then residents of Rochester, purchased a quantity of goods, engaged T. J. Jeffords,[1] a lad of thirteen, as assistant, and made the tour of Indian towns in Western New York. The first camp visited by the traders was located on the ridge, east of Irondequoit bay, and

---

[1] Mr. Jeffords is well known to the citizens of Rochester, having held several positions of honor and trust in the county of Monroe. The pleasure of a visit to his pleasant home in East Rush is greatly enhanced by the presence of his aunt, Mrs. Rebekah Price, the first white child born in Richfield, Otsego county, September 2d, 1791. Mrs. Price has lived at Rush since 1805. Her mind is as clear and active as that of many people at sixty. From the rich store-house of her memory and the recollections of Mr. Jeffords, many interesting facts concerning Indian and pioneer times have been obtained.

consisted largely of French associates of the Indians, with whom they were
living. The second town was on or near the present farm of Judge Edmond
Kelly, south of Irondequoit landing. The traders found about twenty Indians
at the Bell farm on the north side of Honeoye outlet, and one hundred and
fifty at Cannawaugus. Passing through York to Wiscoy above Portage, they
struck a town of three hundred Senecas. At Red House station, above Salamanca, they found four hundred and fifty Indians. On the bank of Silver
creek, near Captain Camp's residence, one hundred Senecas were engaged in
a council.

In his late work, *Weird Legends and Traditions of the Seneca Indians*,
issued in May, 1884, Rev. J. W. Sanborn presents the results of his experience
as a missionary to that nation. Touching the present population of the Indians, chapter XXIV., he says :—

"In Western New York the total population of the Senecas is 3,014, disposed as
follows: On the Alleghany reserve 914, Cattaraugus reserve 1,500, Tonawanda reserve
600. The Indian population, including all the tribes in the state of New York, is fully
6,000."

CHAPTER XIII.[1]

WHEN Oliver Phelps held his treaty with the Indians at Buffalo, in 1788,
he was anxious to secure all their lands within the Massachusetts preëmption claim, but the Indians declined to part with any land west of the
Genesee river, regarding that stream as a natural boundary set by the Great
Spirit between the white and red men. Unable to effect his object by honor-
able purchase, Mr. Phelps appealed to the generosity of the Indians and asked
them for a piece of land west of the Genesee, large enough for a "mill
seat," representing the great convenience a mill would be to them, whereupon the
Indians requested him to state the amount of land required for such a purpose.
Mr. Phelps replied that a piece about twelve miles wide, extending from Cannawaugus (Avon) on the west side of the Genesee river to Lake Ontario, about
twenty-eight miles, would answer his purpose. The Indians were reluctant to
part with so large a tract, but, upon Mr. Phelps's assurance that it was all

---

[1] The material for chapters XIII. and XIV. is derived from the journals of Charlevoix, and Maude,
the *Life of Mary Jemison*, Turner's histories of the *Holland Purchase*, and *Phelps & Gorham Purchase*, *Pioneer Collections*, and private journal of the writer compiled from personal researches.

needed, granted his request. This strip of land, thus acquired by Oliver Phelps, contained about 200,000 acres and was designated the "Genesee Falls mill lot." The first survey of the mill tract was made by Colonel Hugh Maxwell, who started at Cannawaugus, ran twelve miles west of the Genesee river, and then due north to Lake Ontario. Whether these lines were run with a view of again cheating the red men, or were made through mistake is not certain; but the Indians bitterly opposed the boundaries thus created, and Augustus Porter ran a new line which was as near an average of twelve miles from the Genesee as a straight line would permit. In after surveys west of this line, the tract struck out of Maxwell's survey by Porter was termed the "Triangle."

Mr. Phelps fulfilled his agreement with the Indians by a contract with one Ebenezer Allan, who agreed to erect saw and grist mills at the Genesee falls, the consideration being the conveyance to Allan of one hundred acres of land, commencing at the center of the mill and extending an equal distance up and down the river, then west far enough to contain the hundred acres in a square form. So far as known no writings ever passed between Phelps and Allan, but in a deed for twenty thousand acres embracing all the present site of Rochester west of the Genesee river, sold to Quartus Pomeroy, Justin Ely, Ebenezer Hunt and a Mr. Breck in 1790, an exception and reservation was made of "the one hundred acres previously granted to Ebenezer Allan."

Allan is supposed to have been the first white settler in the Genesee valley, other than the tory Walker at the mouth of the Genesee, and first white occupant of the territory now covered by the city of Rochester. Whatever his faults and vices, this fact is patent, and from his first appearance as an actual resident of the Genesee valley dates the era of permanent settlement. No history of Rochester would be complete that omitted mention of Ebenezer Allan and his many interests in Western New York. From the mouth of the river at Lake Ontario to the lower falls at Gardeau, Allan inaugurated improvements which have found their full development only during the present generation. Nearly a century has elapsed since the sounds of his rasping mill-saw first echoed across our beautiful river and were hushed in the roar of untamed waters dashing over their rocky bed in the channel below; but the memory of his presence here, on the soil we love so well, must be cherished while the Flower city has an existence.

In the Revolutionary war Allan was a tory and became acquainted with the Senecas during their incursions against American settlements on the Susquehanna. He joined the Indians in their predatory battles, and excelled all his savage associates in ferocious cruelty. Mary Jemison, the "white woman," says that during one of his scouting expeditions with the Indians Allan entered a house very early in the morning where he found a man, his wife and one child, in bed. The man instantly sprang on the floor for the purpose of defending himself and family; but Allan killed him at one blow, cut off his head and threw it into the bed with the terrified woman; took the child from its mother's breast and dashed its head against the jamb, leaving the unhappy widow and mother alone with her murdered family. It has been said by some that after killing the child Allan opened the fire and buried it under the coals and ashes, but of that Mrs. Jemison was uncertain; though she thought Allan repented these deeds in later days. He accompanied the Senecas to the Genesee, and was with Walker at the battle of Newtown. When the Indians returned to their desolated homes, after the departure of Sullivan's army in the fall of 1779, Mrs. Jemison went to Gardeau and husked corn for two negroes who lived there. In the spring of 1780 she built a house on the flats, and Allan made his appearance at that place soon after. He was apparently without any business to support him, and remained at the white woman's house during the following winter. In the spring Allan commenced working the flats and continued to labor there until the peace of 1783, when he went to Philadelphia, and in a short time returned with a horse loaded with dry goods. Locating on the present site of Mount Morris he built a house and became a trader.

Dissatisfied with the treaty of peace, the British and Indians on the frontier determined to continue their depredations on the white settlements between the Genesee and Albany. The Senecas were about setting out on an expedition when Allan, understanding their mode of warfare, procured a belt of wampum and carried it as a token of peace either to the commander of the nearest American military post, or to the American commissioner. The officer sent word to the Indians that the wampum was cordially accepted and a continuance of peace was ardently desired. The Indians considered the wampum a sacred thing, and dared not go against the import of its meaning. They immediately buried the hatchet as respected the Americans, and smoked the pipe of peace; but with the aid of the British resolved to punish Allan for presenting the wampum without their knowledge. A party of British soldiers was sent from Fort Niagara to apprehend Allan, but he had escaped and they confiscated his property and returned to the fort. A second attempt to capture him failed, as he was concealed in a cave about Gardeau and supplied with food by the white woman; a third effort was successful and Allan was taken to Mont--- ' Quebec for trial, where he was honorably acquitted of the cri--- it is, putting too sudden a stop to the war. Proceeding :hased on credit a boat load of goods, which he brought and thence to Mount Morris on horses provided by ds were exchanged for ginseng and furs, which Allan ing a large crop of corn on his own land, he carried to the mouth of Allen's creek, then called Gin-is- ? he built a house and cultivated the soil. Butler's rangers and the Indians would steal cattle from the Mohawk and the Susquehanna and drive them to the Genesee, where Allan kept them on the rich flats until in prime condition and then sold them at Fort Niagara and in Canada. Col. Butler, British superintendent of Indian affairs at Niagara, supplied Allan with a quantity of goods for the Indian trade, and the latter appropriated the lot to his own use and profit.

In July, 1788, as previously stated, Allan contracted with Mr. Phelps to erect saw and grist mills on the one-hundred-acre lot at the Genesee falls. During the following summer he built the saw-mill and got out timber for a grist mill. At that period the river bed was nearly level from the location of the present aqueduct, south to the race dam at the jail, and the Indian canoe landing was on the present site of W. S. Kimball's tobacco factory. There was a perpendicular fall fourteen feet high, where the aqueduct is located, which was then known as the "upper fall." The ledge of limestone forming this fall curved northwest to the corner of Basin street, where it again turned west and, running nearly parallel with West Main street, ended abruptly about one hundred feet west of Plymouth avenue. This "stone ridge" was from ten to fourteen feet in height. It has been entirely removed above the present surface of the ground, but a portion of its base now forms the west side of the mill race under Aqueduct street. All land east of this ledge to the present channel of the river, is "filled ground." The saw-mill erected by Allan stood upon the present site of the building owned by Nehemiah Osburn, east of Aqueduct street. The first lumber sawed was used to roof the mill, the second was for the grist mill, and the third was sold to Orange Stone.

In the fall of 1789 Peter Sheffer, and his sons Peter and Jacob, came upon the Genesee and found Allan on his farm near the mouth of Allen's creek. He had a comfortable log house on his land, three hundred acres of which had been given him by the Indians, and one hundred and seventy purchased of Phelps and Gorham. Some sixty acres of flats were under cultivation, and twenty then in wheat, while the farm was stocked with horses, cattle, etc. Mr. Sheffer purchased this tract for $2.50 an acre. Turner says that the money realised by the sale of this farm enabled Allan to push forward his mill enterprise, yet he also states that the Sheffers did not reach the Genesee until December. This is evidently a mistake, as the deed from Allan to Peter Sheffer is dated November 23d, 1789, was acknowledged before Timothy Hosmer, November 12th, 1793, and recorded on page 178 book 2 in the county clerk's office at Canandaigua, March 39th, 1794. Furthermore William Hencher stated that the frame of Allan's grist mill was raised November 12th and 13th. That was at an earlier date than Turner supposed Mr. Sheffer to have been in this region.

Allan sent out Indian runners to invite every white man in Genesee val to the raising of the grist mill. The party numbered just fourteen.

The mill frame was heavy, hewed timber, twenty-six by thirty feet. It stood north of the saw-mill previously erected, upon what was afterward known as the "old red mill" site, on "Mill lot number 2." This exact spot is directly in the rear of numbers 39 and 41 East Main street, half way between Aqueduct and Graves street. The ground is now occupied by M. F. Reynolds's paint mill, and E. R. Andrews's printing establishment. Allan procured rum from a trading boat at the mouth of the river, and liquor was "free as water." The entire party camped on the ground the first night. Lumber for the mill floor had been previously sawed and was laid on the 13th, all hands indulging in a dance in the evening and then sleeping on the new floor. The iron for both mills was brought on horseback from Conhocton to Allan's farm, and thence down the river in canoes. In bringing the mill irons down, a Dutchman named Andrews, having them in charge, went over the upper fall and was drowned. The iron was recovered, but Andrews was never seen again, and Allan was credited with his murder.

In August, 1800, John Maude, an English traveler, passed through the lower Genesee country and in his description of the Allan grist mill says : "It contains but one pair of stones made from the stone of a neighboring quarry, which is found to be very suitable for this purpose." This curious statement of Maude's has been repeated by every historian writing on this subject, so far as we are aware, to the present day. The "quarry" mentioned has remained undiscovered thus far (1884), and Mr. Maude's informant led him into other and more serious misstatements, one of which was that said informant "remembered the two steps of the lower falls (some twenty rods apart) as united in one fall. A reference to Charlevoix's description of the Genesee in 1721 shows that the lower falls were then identically the same as at present, as regards distance. The run of stone used in Allan's grist mill were made from boulders on the surface of the ground near the mill. With the assistance of Indians, Allan himself cut and dressed both stones. He was a blacksmith, had a forge near his house at Allen's creek, and also one at the grist mill, where he fitted the mill irons with his own hands. Allan often shod his own horses and repaired guns for himself and the Indians.

With all his faults, Ebenezer Allan was not lazy. He was imposing in appearance, and though usually mild in manner had a bold, determined look and the faculty of controlling all about him. He usually had from ten to thirty Indians at work, and in return supplied them and their families with everything required, including whisky. Wherever Allan went, a company of Indian satellites attended to do his bidding. During his stay at the grist mill the Senecas encamped in the vicinity of Exchange street, and at the Indian spring. He was an adopted member of the Seneca nation, and was known to the red men as Jen-uh-shi-o. From his intimate associations with the natives he was called "Indian Allan" by the whites, who greatly disliked him. About the time of his first appearance on the Genesee, Allan married a Seneca squaw named Kyen-da-nent. Her English name was Sally. They had two daughters, Mary, born in 1780, and Chloe, born March 3d, 1782. While at the falls in 1789 a man named Chapman stopped with his family on their way to Canada, and Allan proposed to the daughter Lucy, to whom he was married by a sham magistrate. Chapman went on his journey to Canada and Lucy was taken back to Allan's farm, where she found his squaw wife and children. About this time Allan beat a boy to death, and pushed an old man into the Genesee, intending to drown him and marry his wife. The man got out of the river, but died next day, and his murderer added the widow to his harem. He also married the half-breed daughter of a negro named Captain Sunfish, and robbed the old man of his money. On his removal to Mount Morris Allan married one Millie McGregor, daughter of an English tory, and is said to have had half a dozen other wives during his residence in the Genesee valley. Lucy Allan had one child, Millie six, and Sally two. Upon the completion of the mill Allan moved into a room in the building, and so far as known his was the first white family that resided on the site of Rochester. Poor as it was, the grist mill proved a benefit to the few settlers in the sparsely inhabited region. People came from Lima, Avon, Victor, Irondequoit and other towns to get a grist or procure a few boards from the saw-mill.

It has been frequently stated that Allan's was the first grist mill in the Genesee valley, but this statement is incorrect. During the winter of 1788–9 John and James Markham built on a little stream which enters the Genesee river about two miles north of Avon. It was a small log building, and all the lumber used in its construction was hewed out by hand. The curbs were hewed plank, the spindle made by straightening out a section of a cart tire, and the stones roughly cut from native rock. There was no bolt, the substitutes being hand sieves made of splints. The mill was a rude, primitive concern, but it mashed corn better than the wooden mortar and pestle then used by early settlers, and during the year or two of its existence was highly valued.

Allan's residence here was temporary. In 1790 he bought a stock of goods in Philadelphia and reopened his trading station at Mount Morris, leaving his brother-in-law, Christopher Dugan, in charge of the mills. Just when Allan moved his family to Mount Morris is not known, but it is probable that they left the mills early in 1792, soon after the sale of the one-hundred-acre lot to Mr. Barton. The deed, or more properly, assignment of his interest, given by Ebenezer Allan to Benjamin Barton, is the foundation of all titles to real estate within the so-called "one-hundred-acre tract," the boundaries of which may be crudely described as running from the jail on the bank of the Genesee about four hundred feet south of Court street, west to a point near Caledonia avenue and Spring street, thence north to an angle about one hundred feet northwest of the corner of Frank and Center streets, and due east to the river

directly east of Market street.   A fac-simile copy of this venerable document
is shown on the next page.   Its subject matter is as follows : —

"Articles of agreement made this 27th day of March in the year of our Lord one
thousand Seven Hundred and Ninety-two, between Ebenezer Allin and Benjamin Barton, witnesseth that for and in Consideration of Five Hundred pounds New York Currency received by the said Ebenezer Allin of Benjamin Barton, the said Ebenezer Allin
doth sell all that Tract of land containing one hundred acres lying on the west side of the
Genesee river in the County of Ontario State of New York Bounded East on the Genesee
river so as to take in the Mills lately Built by the said Allin.   From thence to run Northerly from said Mills Sixty three rods also southerly of said Mills Sixty three rods from
thence Turning westerly so as to make one hundred acres strict measure.   And the said
Ebenezer Allin doth hereby impower the said Benjamin Barton to apply to the Honr'd
Oliver Phelps and Nathaniel Gorham or Either of them for a good and sufficient deed of
conveyance to be by them — or Either of them executed to the said Benjamin Barton,
his Heirs or assigns for said Tract of land and the said Ebenezer Allin doth hereby
request and Impower the said Oliver Phelps or Nathaniel Gorham to seale and Deliver
such Deed to the said Benjamin Barton his Heirs or assigns, and the said Ebenezer
Allin doth hereby exonerate and discharge the said Oliver Phelps and Nathaniel Gorham
in consequence of their executing the deed ass'd, from all and Every agreement or Instrument which might or may have existed Respecting the conveyance of said Tract of land
from them the said Oliver Phelps and Nathaniel Gorham or Either of them to the said
Ebenezer Allin, in Witness whereof the said Ebenezer Allin hath hereunto set his Hand
and Seal the day and year above written.

"Sealed and delivered
     in the presense off   "E. ALLAN [seal]
Gertrude G Ogden
John Farlin"

"Recd. of Benjamin Barton a Deed for Allens Mills on the Genesee River, in
settling therefor I am to settle the Bond for £300 which he gave Ebenezer Allen for
which I was security.   Dec. 24th 1793.   SAML. OGDEN."

"Contract for Deed
of Rochester Land.

———

Ebenezer Allen
Alias Indian Allen,
To
Benjamin Barton
1792

This is the foundation
of Allens Mills
John Barton, son
of Benjamin, says
his father paid
Allen $200. for
this 100 acres."[1]

——— — ———

[1] This indorsement was made by Mr. Turner.

Articles of agreement made this 21st day of March in the year of our Lord one thousand Seven Hundred and Ninety two between Ebenezer Allen and Benjamin in Barton. Witnesseth that for and in Consideration of Five Hundred pounds New york Currency paid by the said Ebenezer Allen of Benjamin Barton the said Ebenezer Allen doth sell all that tract of Land containing one hundred acres lying on the west side of the Genesee River in the County of Ontario State of New York Bounded East on the Genesee River so as to take in the Mills lately Built by the said Allen, So or thence to run Northerly from said Mills Sixty three Rods also one Thirty of said mills Sixty three Rods from thence running westerly so as to make one hundred acres strict Measure And the said Ebenezer Allen doth hereby impower the said Benjamin Barton to apply to the Hon'ble Oliver Phelps and Nathaniel Gorham or Either of them for a good and Sufficient deed of conveyance to be by them or — Either of them executed to the said Benjamin Barton, his Heirs or Assigns for said Tract of Land and the said Ebenezer Allen doth hereby request and Impower the said Oliver Phelps or Nathaniel Gorham to seal Execute and Deliver such deed to the said Benjamin Barton his Heirs or Assigns. and the said Ebenezer Allen doth hereby exonerate and discharge the said Oliver Phelps and Nathaniel Gorham in consequence of their executing the deed afs'd from all and every agreement or Instrument which might or may have existed respecting the conveyance of said Tract

of Land from them the said Oliver Phelps and
Nathaniel Gorham or Either of them to the said
Ebenezer Allin in Witness whereof the said Ebenezer
Allen hath hereunto set his Hand and Seal the
day and year above written

Sealed and delivered
in the Presence of —
Gertrude G Ogden
John Farlow

E Allen

Contract for Deed
of Rochester Land,
Ebenezer Allen
alias Indian Allen
To
Benjamin Barton
1792

This is the foundation
of Albert title

John Barton for
Benjamin Day,
Benjamin Barton,
Allen $200/½
was 100 acres,

This deed has a curious history. Its existence appears to have passed from public memory until Orsamus Turner began the collection of material for his grand histories of the Phelps & Gorham and Holland purchases. During a visit to the family residence of Brandt, the noted Mohawk sachem, at Brantford, Ontario, Mr. Turner found the Allan deed, among other papers formerly belonging to Brandt, stored in a barrel in the garret. No information could be obtained regarding the time or manner in which Brandt came into possession of the document, which was readily given to Mr. Turner. In June, 1849, he requested D. M. Dewey to present the old deed to the Rochester Athenæum for safe keeping. It passed into the possession of M. F. Reynolds, with other effects of the Athenæum, and is now carefully treasured in the Reynolds library.

Soon after his return to Mount Morris, Allan induced the Seneca chiefs to give a tract of land four miles square, where he then resided, to his half-breed daughters for their support and education.[1] He artfully framed the conveyance so that he could appropriate the land to his own use, but, in accordance with its provisions, sent his Indian girls to a school at Trenton, New Jersey; also sending his white son to Philadelphia, to obtain an English education. In 1792 Allan built a saw-mill on the outlet of Silver lake, at Smoky hollow, near the Genesee river. He sold the land deeded to his girls to Robert Morris, and removed them from school. In 1797 Allan disposed of all his property in the Genesee valley and removed to Delawaretown, in Upper Canada, leaving his squaw wife behind. He also arranged with two men to drown his white wife, Millie. The men brought her down the river in a canoe and purposely ran the boat over the upper fall, but Millie escaped to the shore and followed Allan to Canada. Governor Simcoe granted him three thousand acres of land upon condition of certain improvements, and Allan became rich. In 1806 his white neighbors combined against him, and he was repeatedly arrested upon charges of forgery, larceny, etc., but was invariably acquitted. Losses of property followed, and about 1814 Allan died in greatly reduced circumstances, willing all his interest to Millie and her children. About 1820 a son of Ebenezer Allan came to Rochester and set up a claim for his mother's right of dower in the One-hundred-acre tract. It will be seen, by reference to the conveyance given to Barton, that Allan's name alone is attached to the instrument. A compromise was effected with parties holding titles in the property, but our informant, the venerable Mrs. Abelard Reynolds, has too indistinct a remembrance of the affair to aid us with particulars.

---

[1] This deed was recorded in the office of the clerk of Ontario county, at Canandaigua, August 1st, 1791, in book of deeds number 1, page 134. It was signed by eighteen sachems, chiefs and warriors of the Seneca nation, So-go-u-a-ta, better known as "Red Jacket," being of the number.

MR. BARTON sold the One-hundred-acre tract to Samuel B. Ogden, December 24th, 1793. The latter transferred the property to Charles Williamson, of Bath, agent for Sir William Pulteney, and it thus became a part of the Pulteney estate. Upon his removal to Mount Morris, Allan placed his brother-in-law, Christopher Dugan, in charge of the mills, and Dugan's was the second family on the site of Rochester. Allan's sister is said to have been a lady of education and culture, who married an old British soldier, and followed her wayward brother to the wilderness, where she clung to him through all his wickedness for years. She became housekeeper for her brother, and with her husband formed a part of Allan's family until the latter left the mills. August 9th, 1794, Dugan wrote to Colonel Williamson, saying : —

"The mill erected by Ebenezer Allan, which I am informed you have purchased, is in a bad situation, much out of repair, and, unless attention is paid to it, it will soon take its voyage to the lake. I have resided here for several years, and kept watch and ward without fee or recompense ; and am pleased to hear that it has fallen into the hands of a gentleman who is able to repair it, and whose character is such that I firmly believe he will not allow an old man to suffer without reward for his exertions. I wish to have you come or send some one to take care of the mill, as my situation is such as makes it necessary soon to remove."

Mr. Dugan left the mill soon after, and settled on his farm near Dugan's creek. At the time of Aaron Burr's visit to the Genesee falls, the following summer, not a soul could be found about this vicinity.

In 1795 Colonel Josiah Fish purchased a farm at the mouth of Black creek and with the aid of his son Lebbeus commenced improvements. They came down to the falls late in the season and boarded with a man named Sprague, whom they found in charge of the Allan mills. The fare consisted of "raccoon for breakfast, dinner and supper, with no vegetables. On extra occasions cakes, fried in raccoon oil, were added." It would thus appear that Sprague was the third resident of Rochester, though no mention was made of his family. In 1796 Mr. Williamson expended about five hundred dollars in improvements at the falls, and engaged Colonel Fish to take charge of the mills. The latter moved his family, consisting of his wife, a son and one daughter, here in November. They did their cooking in a board shanty which was built against the stone ledge at the present northwest corner of Basin and Aqueduct streets, and resided in the grist mill, which was minus glass windows and other comforts. The next fall Colonel Fish put up three sides of a log house against the stone ledge, which constituted the back wall, in which a chimney-place was excavated. Turner says this house stood on the site of the old red mill near

Child's basin. It has been assumed that he was in error, but one fact appears to be overlooked, or is unknown to certain writers; there were two "Red" mills, the second one occupying the present (1884) site of the Arcade mills on the east side of Aqueduct street. The ruins of a log house remained there in 1812, and Turner had reference to this spot. Colonel Fish was the fourth resident of Rochester, and the house erected by him was the first building occupied exclusively as a dwelling, within the present bounds of the Flower city. When Thomas Morris escorted Louis Philippe, afterward king of France, and his brothers, the Duke de Montpensier and Count Beaujolais, from Canandaigua to view the Genesee falls in 1797, they entirely overlooked the humble dwelling at the mills; but in 1800 a party bound up the lake, of which William Nixon Loomis was one, were overtaken by a storm off the mouth of the Genesee and, running into the river for safety, came up to view the falls. "Upon the present site of Rochester they came to a solitary log cabin, knocked and were bid to come in. Upon entering they found that in the absence of the family a parrot had been the hospitable representative. The family (Col. Fish's) returned soon, however, and gave them a supper of potatoes and milk." In 1798-9 Jeremiah Olmstead moved to the falls and lived in a hut south of the House of Refuge. This shanty had been erected by one Farewell, who remained there but a short time. He was the fifth resident of Rochester and Olmstead the sixth, so far as is known, but future researches may change the order of succession. Turner says the clearing made by Olmstead "was the first blow struck in the way of improvement, other than the Allan mill, on all the present site of the city of Rochester." In 1800 Oliver Culver purchased a farm on what is now East avenue and the Culver road, cleared seven acres and sowed it to wheat. Suspecting that his title was imperfect, Mr. Culver left the farm until 1805, when he returned and became a permanent settler. He was the seventh resident within the present boundaries of Rochester. The same year Wheelock Wood, of Lima, built a saw-mill on Deep hollow, and operated it one year, but the terrible fever and ague, the enemy of all early settlers, prostrated his workmen and forced Mr. Wood to abandon the place. He is supposed to have been the eighth resident. In the journal of his visit to Western New York in 1800, John Maude says that on August 19th he arrived at "Genesee Mills."

"As Colonel Fish, the miller, had not those accommodations which I expected, not even a stable, I was obliged to proceed to Mr. King's at the Genesee landing, where I got a good breakfast on wild pigeons, etc. Mr. King is the only respectable settler in this township (number 1 short range) in which there are at present twelve families, four of them at the landing. . . . . Further improvements are much checked in consequence of the titles to the lands here being in dispute. Mr. Phelps sold three thousand acres in this neighborhood to Mr. Granger for ten thousand dollars, secured by mortgage on the land. Granger died soon after his removal here, and, having sold part of the land, the residue would not clear the mortgage, which prevented his heirs administering the estate. Phelps foreclosed the mortgage, and entered on possession, even on that part which had been sold and improved. Some settlers, in consequence, quitted their farms; others repaid the purchase money; and others are endeavoring to make some accommodation with Mr. Phelps. . . . . . The landing is four miles from the mouth of the river, where two log huts are built at the entrance to Lake Ontario. . . . . . At noon returned in company with Colonel Fish. Had a fine view from the top of the bank, of the lower falls, of which I took a sketch. The lower fall is fifty-four feet, the middle fall ninety-six feet, and the upper fall must be something under thirty feet. . . . . . In a few minutes I joined Colonel Fish at the Mills. . . . . . The grist mill is very ill-constructed; it is too near the bed of the river, and the race so improperly managed that it is dry in summer and liable to back-water in winter. This mill is not at present able to grind more than ten bushels a day ; were it in good order it would grind sixty. It is now almost entirely neglected, in consequence of being so much out of repair. The saw-mill is already ruined."

In 1802 Colonel Fish returned to his farm at Black creek, and after his departure the Allan grist mill had no regular miller. It was nominally in charge of a Mr. King, who came from Hanford's landing and lived in a shanty just west of the middle falls. Occasionally one or two settlers would make necessary repairs and grind their own grists free of cost. In 1804 Noah Smith built a mill for Tryon and Adams on Allen's creek in Brighton. This mill was located on the west side of the stream, about twenty rods north of the present New York Central railway embankment. Oliver Griswold of Irondequoit landing purchased the old Allan mill stones and irons for Tryon and Adams, who placed them in the new mill. In 1803 the Allan saw-mill was swept away in a freshet which broke over the race gate and undermined the building, nearly carrying the grist mill also. This was destroyed by fire in 1807. In 1806 Solomon Fuller built a small mill on Irondequoit creek, and the Allan stones and irons are said to have been transferred to that mill. They passed into the possession of Lyman Goff, who sold them to Stephen Chubb. The latter used them in a horse-mill in Henrietta. In 1825 Isaac Barnes and Captain Enos Blossom built a grist mill on the west bank of Allen's creek about thirty rods north of East avenue. These gentlemen bought the Allan stones of Mr. Chubb, and placed them in their mill, with one other run of stone. The mill was rebuilt in 1837, and the old stones were taken to Mr. Barnes's residence, where they were used as door steps for many years. In 1859 Lorenzo D. Ely and Oliver Culver reported to the Junior Pioneer association of Rochester, that the Allan mill stones were in the possession of Isaac Barnes, and his son Charles Milo Barnes, millers at Allen's creek, and suggested the propriety of securing these valuable historical relics of Rochester's first settler. Oliver Culver, Lyman Goff and Mr. and Mrs. Isaac Barnes fully identified the stones as the original run made and used by Indian Allan. They consisted of the bed and running stone, and were too large and heavy to place in an ordinary room. A petition was presented to the board of supervisors of Monroe county, in December, and that body passed a resolution that "the Junior Pioneer society have leave to place in the rear of the court-house a pair of mill stones said to have been the first ever used in this county." [1]   In order to defray the expense of removing the stones to Rochester, a subscription list was circulated by Jarvis M. Hatch between the 4th and 15th of February, 1860.   It was signed by S. W. D. Moore, Samuel Richardson, Charles J. Hill, Thomas Kempshall, L. A. Ward, Joseph Field, William Pitkin, John B. Elwood, N. E. Paine, Rufus Keeler, Charles H. Clark, John Williams, E. F. Smith, Isaac Hills, Jonathan Child, sr., Hamlin Stilwell, Maltby Strong, C. J. Hayden and Jacob Gould, each of whom agreed to pay one dollar.   The Messrs. Barnes generously donated the mill stones to the Junior Pioneer association, and Charles M. Barnes brought them to the city.   A committee from the association received and placed the stones in the rear of the court-house.   At the building of the new city hall, south of the court-house, the old mill stones were used as foundations for two lamp-posts at the entrance to the city hall.   It would be a fitting and proper action for our city authorities to remove the valuable relics to a permanent and secure place where they will be preserved for future generations.

In 1802 Nathaniel Rochester, William Fitzhugh and Charles Carroll bought the One-hundred-acre lot of Sir William Pulteney's agent, for seventeen and one half dollars per acre.   Having greater interests elsewhere, the proprietors took no steps to improve or settle the tract until 1810.   At the date of purchase the special interest of new settlers in this vicinity was centered in Tryon's Town, south of Irondequoit landing, and King's (now Hanford's) landing, near the lower falls.   It was thought by shrewd men that one of those places would in time become the great business center of the lower Genesee country. James Wadsworth succeeded to the agency of the Pulteney estate and, becoming part owner of a tract on the west side of the river near the Rapids, made strenuous efforts to found a city there.   The place was named "Castle Town" or Castleton, in honor of a resident, Colonel Isaac Castle.   A tavern, store and other business was started, and several people located there, but the "city" was a failure.   The hundred-acre tract was then termed "Fall Town," and the superior water privileges of this immediate vicinity, combined with other advantages of the location, eventually drew the strength of public opinion in its favor, while the indomitable spirit and enterprise of its pioneer inhabitants laid the foundation for our present magnificent city.   Elijah Rose settled on the east side of the river in 1806, and built a log house on Mount Hope avenue, (the present street number of which is 281), about one hundred and fifty feet south of the present residence of George Ellwanger.   This house was subsequently occupied by several families—those of Jacob Miller, Daniel Harris, John Nutt and other pioneers.   The writer has often heard his aged grandmother

---

[1] For the verification of this fact, and much valuable information regarding the period of early settlement, we are indebted to Donald McNaughton, whose father, John McNaughton, was one of the first pioneers west of the Genesee.

and her sister, the late Mrs. Lucretia Lee, relate their experience in fighting a lot of wolves away from the blanket door of this same log house, about the time of the British invasion at Charlotte, when the men were all absent.

In 1807 Charles Harford erected a block-house near the great falls. It is variously located on State street near Vincent place, and at the intersection of Center and Mill streets. It is said to have been the first well-constructed dwelling in the city limits on the west side of the Genesee. The next year Mr. Harford built a saw-mill, and completed a grist mill on the present location of the Phœnix mill. His mill-race was the beginning of Brown's race. In 1807–8 Lyman Shumway put up a shanty near the falls on the east side of the river; and Samuel Ware came in about 1808–9. In 1788–9 General Hyde, Prosper Polly, Enos Stone, Job Gilbert, and Joseph Chaplin, of Lenox, Massachusetts, and John Lusk, of Berkshire, bought a large tract east of the Genesee, of Phelps and Gorham. In the summer of 1789 Mr. Lusk settled his land at the head of Irondequoit bay, and in the spring of 1790 brought out his family. Enos Stone's son, Orange, Joel Scudder, Chauncey and Calvin Hyde, and others having families, followed soon after. Orange Stone located half a mile east of Brighton village on the Pittsford road, near the "big rock and tree," and opened a tavern. His brother, Enos Stone, jr., with other young men, drove the stock of the new settlers to Brighton, but continued to reside at Lenox for a number of years. He made several visits to the Genesee, and became an agent for the sale of lands. In compensation for his services he received one hundred and fifty acres on the east bank of the river, opposite the hundred-acre tract on the west side. Enos Stone, sr., did not make Rochester his permanent home until 1816, but in 1808 he erected a saw-mill for his son, about one hundred feet north of the east end of the present aqueduct. A freshet afterward carried the mill away. Early in March, 1810, Jacob Miller arrived at the Genesee, and was temporarily domiciled in the log-house built by Mr. Rose. As soon as his house could be made ready, Mr. Miller settled on his farm directly west of the Monroe county penitentiary, and several of his children soon after located in that neighborhood. Enos Stone, jr., also arrived in March, with his family and effects. Mr. Stone made his home at the house of his brother Orange, for several weeks, and during that period a son, James S. Stone, was born May 4th, 1810. The latter now resides on his farm in the town of Greece, hale and hearty at the age of seventy-four.

While staying with his brother, Enos Stone erected a log-house east of the saw-mill, which was rebuilt. In October he put up a small frame building sixteen by twenty feet. The cutting of the timber, raising and inclosing occupied three days, and Mrs. Stone, a hired man and a hired girl assisted. The site of this building was established by Schuyler Moses and Edwin Scrantom several years ago. It was on the east side of South St. Paul street, directly east of the terminus of the aqueduct, and was the first framed dwelling in Rochester. It was removed to number 53 Elm street, where the original timber frame is, covered with modern boards, and the building used as a wood-shed.

CHAPTER XV.

THE ROCHESTER POST-OFFICE.

PRIOR to 1812 the main route from Canandaigua to the Niagara frontier was by the "Buffalo road," which ran through Bloomfield, Avon, Caledonia and other towns westward. In all that portion of New York between this road and Lake Ontario not a single post-office or mail route had been established. In the early season of that year Dr. Levi Ward received authority from Gideon Granger, then postmaster-general, to transport a weekly mail from Caledonia, *via* Riga, Murray, Parma and Northampton, to Charlotte. According to the terms of the contract the mail was to leave Caledonia every Monday morning at eight o'clock, and arrive at Charlotte, a distance of about thirty-two miles, at four p. m. Tuesday. The postmaster-general agreed to appoint deputy postmasters in locations designated by the contractor, which were seven miles distant from each other. Dr. Ward's compensation was the net proceeds of letter and newspaper postage collected on the route. The rate was from twenty to twenty-five cents per letter, according to distance, and for newspapers one cent each. The plan was at once put in operation, and the success and satisfaction resulting induced the postmaster-general to enter into a new contract with Dr. Ward, for the extension of routes along the Ridge road to Oak Orchard creek; from Parma through Ogden and Riga to Bergen, and from Bergen to Batavia; in fact, the arrangement gave Dr. Ward discretionary "authority to designate the location of post-offices wherever he would agree to deliver mail once a week, for all the postage he might collect, in nearly all the country between Canandaigua and the Niagara river, and from the Canandaigua and Buffalo road northward to Lake Ontario."[1] The system continued in operation, supplying the convenience of mail facilities to a wide, sparsely populated region until 1815, and on some of the routes until 1820, when it was generally superseded by the ordinary contract system.

As early as 1804 the business men of Canandaigua contributed to the improvement of a road that had been constructed many years before from Canandaigua to the crossing of Allen's creek on East avenue and thence north to Tryon's Town near Irondequoit landing, and extended it northwest through

---

[1] *Sketches of Rochester.* 1838, by Henry O'Rielly, p. 331.

the present town of Irondequoit, passing in the rear of Hooker's cemetery (where the old road-bed still exists) and across the country to the east bank of the Genesee river and Charlotte, or Port Genesee, as the place was variously termed. All travel from Canandaigua, north of the Buffalo road, was over this so-called "Merchants' road" to Charlotte, and mail matter was occasionally carried by teamsters. In 1812 the latter place was looked upon as the future great lake port and rising town of Western New York,[1] but no means of regular communication existed between that place and Rochester until 1814, when Gideon Cobb started a semi-weekly ox-team line for the conveyance of freight and passengers.

On the establishment of Dr. Ward's postal system F. Bushnell was appointed postmaster at Charlotte, and through the kindness of individuals who "called for mail," the residents of Rochester — numbering fifteen people all told, July 4th, 1812 — were enabled to correspond with the world at large, and receive news *via* Canandaigua or Bath, Avon, Caledonia, Parma and Charlotte. This roundabout course was not considered a sufficient accommodation, and the subject of direct mail connections with the east was earnestly discussed. The late Edwin Scrantom (whose record of early local events is invaluable) was authority for the statement that "the first mail received in Rochester arrived in July, 1812." If the date is correct the mail must have been carried by private individuals during that summer, as no post-office existed and the first postmaster, Abelard Reynolds, was not appointed until October, and his commission not issued until November 19th, 1812.[2] For this appointment Mr. Reynolds was indebted to the influence of Colonel Rochester, through Henry Clay, his intimate friend, and son-in-law of Colonel Thomas Hart, the business partner of Colonel Rochester. It was agreed upon during an interview between Colonel Rochester and Mr. Reynolds, held at Dansville some time in July, 1812; no regular application for a post-office in Rochester had been made to the department at that time.

While here in July Mr. Reynolds purchased lots 23 and 24 north side of Buffalo street, built the wall and frame of a dwelling twenty-four by thirty-six feet, upon lot 23 (now numbered 10, 12, 14, 16, East Main street), contracted for the completion of the house, and late in August returned to Pittsfield, Mass., for his family. In his unpublished memoirs Mr. Reynolds refers to his appointment as postmaster, in the modest manner peculiar to himself: —

"While in the post-office at Pittsfield, in October, Colonel Danforth, the postmaster, informed me that he saw by the papers that I had been appointed postmaster at Rochester. I replied that I had not heard of it, but it was not an unexpected event, as an office had been applied for at that place and my name recommended as a proper person to discharge its duties."

[1] Memoirs of Abelard Reynolds.
[2] Records of Post-Office Department, Washington.

Learning that the contractor had done nothing to his house, Mr. Reynolds engaged Otis Walker of Brighton, to carry himself and a load of furniture to Rochester, where he arrived November 1st. He at once set about the erection of a building on lot 24 (now numbered 18, 20, 22, East Main street) which was completed January 15th. Returning to Massachusetts he engaged William Strong to bring a load of furniture, and with his own horse and cutter brought to their new home his wife, their son William, and Mrs. Reynolds's sister Huldah Strong, arriving at Rochester early in February. Mr. Reynolds was a saddler and occupied the front room of his house for business purposes. There the citizens of Rochester and other early settlers of the vicinity came for their mail.

Among the furniture brought from Pittsfield was a large desk of pine, three and a half feet in length, two wide and four feet high. It had a pigeon-hole compartment in the top and two large drawers underneath furnished with neat brass ring-pulls; it was stained to resemble black walnut, and the sloping top was covered with black velvet trimmed with brass-headed tacks. This desk was placed in the shop, where it served a triple purpose as the receptacle of tools and private and public papers. All mail matter received was put in the pigeon-holes, and practically the desk was the first post-office of Rochester. It was in constant use as the depository of mail and post-office papers during Mr. Reynolds's term of office, and now occupies an honored position in the Reynolds library, firm and substantial as when first made, though plainly exhibiting the marks of over seventy-two years of service. A cut of the desk supplements this chapter.

The first regular mail was brought to Rochester from Canandaigua on horseback. It was received once a week, and part of the time a woman (whose name history fails to reveal) performed the duty of post-rider. The letters were carried in saddle-bags which hung across the horse in rear of the saddle, to which they were attached, and the old mail saddle-bags were usually well filled. The completion of the bridge at Main street in Rochester opened up a shorter route from Canandaigua to the Niagara river, and diverted considerable of the through travel from the Buffalo road passing through Avon and Caledonia. The road from Rochester to Buffalo, via Batavia, was not then opened, and the ridge road between Rochester and Lewiston was simply a wide trail, at times nearly impassable. In 1813 the legislature granted five thousand dollars for "cutting out the path and bridging the streams," and the improved conditions turned the tide of western travel through Rochester, and over the Ridge road, in a steadily increasing flow. During the summer and fall of 1813 Mr. Reynolds finished the basement story and some of the rooms of the large house and moved into it, transferring the post-office business to his new habitation, where the desk previously described continued in service as the regular depository of all mail matter. In 1815 J. G. Bond and Captain Elisha Ely determined to run a stage between Rochester and Canandaigua, and organised a company for that purpose, consisting of William Hildreth of Pittsford, and other tavern-keepers along the route. Mr. Hildreth put a light wagon on the road in November, 1815, the post-rider discontinued his trips, and the mail was carried to and from Rochester by wagon twice a week.

In January, 1816, the company placed a coach body on runners, and it was the first four-in-hand mail coach that ever entered Rochester, the enthusiastic reception accorded to it by the villagers nearly reaching the proportions of a public celebration. Messrs. Bond and Ely extended their enterprise to the Niagara river, by enlisting the tavern-keepers along the Ridge road, their principal supporters and earnest co-laborers being Messrs. Barton and Fairbanks of Lewiston. In the early spring of 1816 General Micah Brooks presented a resolution to congress, inquiring "as to the expediency of establishing a post route from the village of Canandaigua, by way of the village of Rochester, to the village of Lewiston in the county of Niagara and state of New York." The mail was then carried by stage, the company taking all postage received in payment. Congress soon after authorised the route proposed by General Brooks, and the company contracted to carry the mail for a set price. A tri-weekly four-horse coach was put upon the route in June, 1816, and within a year there was often a necessity for sending out three and four extras a day for passengers. The travel increased to such an extent that for several years coaches ran in such numbers that they were seldom out of sight of each other along every mile of the Ridge road.

In 1815 Mr. Reynolds opened his house as a tavern, and in 1817 rented it to Lebbeus Elliot for two years. During that time the post-office remained in the same building, to which Mr. Reynolds returned in the spring of 1819. He added a wing to the east side of the building for a bar-room, with a portico in front, at the east end of which he located the post-office, connecting it with the bar-room. The partition between the office and open part of the portico consisted of a glazed, pigeon-holed case for mail, and the delivery was through an opening in this case to the portico. Persons could thus step from the street into the portico, obtain their mail and pass onward without entering the tavern. The steamer Ontario commenced her trips from Sackett's Harbor to Lewiston in 1817, and once a week came to Hanford's Landing. The postmaster-general having authorised the carrying of mails by steamboats in 1815, the American lake ports and Canada were thus brought into regular communication with Rochester. In 1819 a mail route was established between Cuylerville and Rochester, and in 1820 mails were received once a week from Bath, Dansville, Geneseo, Avon and intermediate towns. It is said that mails from Canandaigua and Lewiston reached Rochester daily in 1820; but "as late as 1821 there was not a single post coach in the United States west of Buffalo. The Erie canal was staked out but not a shovelful of earth had been removed from its bed in Buffalo, railroads were unborn and telegraphs unthought of." [1]

[1] Doty's *History of Livingston County*, p. 597.

In 1824 the mail stage between Rochester and Geneseo ran three times a week each way, leaving here Mondays, Wednesdays and Fridays at half-past five in the morning. In April, 1825, E. Fiske established a daily line of stages from Geneseo, "intersecting the east and west lines at Avon, thus giving daily communication with Rochester, Canandaigua and Batavia." Elegant coaches were placed on the route in December, but the regular mail was carried only three times a week. In 1826 the citizens of Rochester regularly received through the post-office twenty-six daily, two hundred and eighty-four semi-weekly and six hundred and ninety weekly newspapers, and the receipts of the last quarter of that year were $1,718.44. Mails arrived and departed as follows: "Eastern and western, once a day; Palmyra, seven mails a week in summer and three in winter; Penfield, six mails a week; Scottsville, seven mails a week in summer, and three in winter; Oswego, one mail a week; Batavia, three mails a week; Geneseo, three mails a week." Preparatory to the erection of the Arcade, in 1828, the post-office effects were removed to a building on the northwest corner of Buffalo and Hughes streets, now West Main and North Fitzhugh. In the spring Mr. Reynolds moved the tavern building about one hundred and fifty feet north of its original position, and upon the erection of the Arcade it was attached to and constituted the rear part of that structure. In 1829 the post-office was re-established in the new building, on the old location.

To trace the opening of new routes and lines of postal communication between Rochester and the outside world, to record the successive changes in the mode of conveyance from the saddle-bagged post-horse, picking his way through the dangers of a primitive wilderness at the rate of one mile an hour, to the finely appointed mail car of the modern railway, passing through the country over its smooth track of steel at a speed exceeding sixty miles an hour, would require the space of volumes. To chronicle the innovations of time and postal reforms from the uncovered, wafer-sealed sheet requiring twenty-five cents to carry it a distance of one hundred miles, to this era of cheap postage, free delivery and instantaneous postal telegraphic connections around the globe, is not my purpose.

The records of seventy-two years of postal transactions show that political preferment effected many changes in the head of the Rochester post-office. Abelard Reynolds, the pioneer postmaster, commissioned November 19th, 1812, held the position seventeen years, his son William A. Reynolds acting as assistant and deputy during the latter part of his term. Mr. Reynolds's successors, and the dates of their appointment, were as follows: John B. Elwood, June 29th, 1829; Henry O'Rielly, May 24th, 1838; Samuel G. Andrews, January 18th, 1842; Henry Campbell, July 18th, 1845; Darius Perrin, April 12th, 1849; Hubbard S. Allis, June 30th, 1853; Nicholas E. Paine, July 6th, 1858; Scott W. Updike, July 26th, 1861, and July 12th, 1865; John W. Stebbins,

March 28th, 1867; Edward M. Smith, January 16th, 1871; Daniel T. Hunt, March 11th, 1875; March 3d, 1879, and March 3d, 1883.

The changes made in the location of the post-offices have been few. In a letter written to Postmaster-General Barry, April 18th, 1833, Mr. Reynolds inclosed a plan of the Arcade and among other things said : —

"The first room[1] on the west side of the hall, as you enter from Buffalo street, is the post-office. It has a small recess in front, which is closed at night, where the citizens receive their letters and papers. The whole arrangement is admirably calculated to accommodate the public, the Arcade hall being sufficiently spacious to contain all who will ever congregate on the arrival of the mail."

The rapid increase in population, however, exceeded even Mr. Reynolds's expectations, and he soon after made arrangements for a better accommodation of the post-office and the public. The old tavern post-office building was removed from the rear of the Arcade to the north side of Bugle alley (Exchange place), where Corinthian Academy of Music now stands, and in 1848 was moved to numbers 11 and 13, Sophia street. There the frame was bricked up and in its new form the building has been in use as a private residence to the present day. Upon its former site, in the rear of the Arcade, Abelard Reynolds erected a brick building, forty-six by twenty-two feet. This stood fifteen feet north of the Arcade, to which it was connected by a frame building, or covered-way and was used solely for postal purposes. It extended to Exchange place, and walks along each side afforded free passage through the Arcade to Main street. About 1842 this post-office building was torn down, the Arcade extended to Exchange place, and the post-office located at the northwest end of the hall. In 1859 it was removed to the east side. To meet the requirements of increasing business additional space has been acquired from time to time, until the post-office now includes 15, 17, 19 Arcade hall, 37, 39 Arcade gallery and 11 to 23 inclusive, Exchange place, covering an area of floor room exceeding 8,000 square feet.

A comparative statement of postal statistics will illustrate the wonderful changes that have occurred during the span of a single life and within the memory of many persons now living. The population of Rochester January 1st, 1813, did not exceed fifty people, all told. The mail, then averaging about four pieces, arrived and departed once a week after that date, and the receipts of the post-office for the first quarter of the year were $3.42, the expense and profit to the government nothing. Until 1819 all mail matter was kept in a desk, and for a period of twenty years following its establishment the duties of the office were performed by the postmaster and one assistant

January 1st, 1884, the population of Rochester numbered 108,971. Mails were received daily by twenty-two railway trains and six stage routes; the letter pouches and sacks received averaging 119 and those dispatched 379.

---

[1] No. 4, present Arcade hall.

The number of pieces handled by carriers during 1883 was 12,891,375. The number of pieces handled daily by the entire office force averaged 100,000, and the aggregate for the year was 36,000,000. The total transactions of the money order department were 100,695 amounting to $863,751.92. The registry department registered 12,754 letters and 4,034 packages, and delivered at the office 48,870 letters. The gross sum received by the post-office in 1883 was $259,840.13; the total expense $57,466.41, leaving a net profit to the government of $202,373.72.

The officials of the office were: Postmaster, Daniel T. Hunt; assistant postmaster, W. Seward Whittlesey; superintendent of carriers, George F. Loder; assistant superintendent of carriers, James T. Sproat; chief clerk, Calvin Wait; money order department, Willis G. Mitchell; registry department, Frank A. Bryan; stamp department, Jacob G. Maurer; mailing department, William C. Walker; assisted by a force of twenty-five clerks and thirty-three letter carriers.

Note.—All of the foregoing chapters were prepared by Mr. George H. Harris.—[ED.

THE FIRST POST-OFFICE OF ROCHESTER.

Root Foods

Seneca Indians.

Root Foods

of the

Seneca Indians.

By

GEO. H. HARRIS,

Rochester, N. Y.

·—

Published by the Society,

Rochester, N. Y.,

July, 1891.

ROOT FOODS OF THE SENECA INDIANS.

By Geo. H. Harris.

A complete history of the foods of the aborigines of North America would fill volumes. The list comprises nearly all indigenous vegetation including grass, seeds, leaves, barks and roots ; all game animals, and many not usually eaten, as reptiles, insects and mollusks. We take into special consideration the root foods of the Seneca Indians who, but a century ago, possessed the magnificent domain their pale-faced successors denominate Western New York.

The Seneca was one of five separate nations that, about the middle of the fifteenth century, united in a confederacy termed by later white men the League of-the Iroquois ; the territory of the confederated nations covering the present State of New York from the Hudson River to the Genesee, and by later conquest extending west and south of Lake Erie.

The mythology of the Iroquois assigns their creation to Hä-wen-né-yu, a Good Spirit who, with his brother Ha-ne-go-até-geh, an Evil minded spirit, once ruled the world. The Good Spirit created all useful animals and products of the earth : while the Evil Spirit created all monsters, poisonous reptiles, and noxious plants. To assist them in their labors Hä-wen-né-yu and Ha-ne-go-até-geh created classes of subordinate spirits and committed to each the care of some particular thing. Every object in nature had its protecting spirit. Those spirits created by Ha-wen-né-yu were termed Ho-no-che-nó-keh, or the Invisible Aids. They were the guardians of fire, water, medicine, and all species of trees, shrubs, and plants, that bore good fruit or were beneficial to man. The spirits subordinate to Ha-ne-go-até-geh were, like their creator, antagonistic to all good things. They were the spirits of all plants and roots of a poisonous nature, the progenitors of witches and enchanters, and destroyed men with disease and pestilence.

Possessing a perfect knowledge of the topography of their vast territory, the Iroquois selected for their summer homes the open glades of the forest or the alluvial bottoms of the numerous valleys, where their crude efforts in cultivating the rich soils were repaid by abundant crops. When, in 1687 De Nonville, the French governor of Canada, came to Irondequoit bay and destroyed the Seneca towns, he was astounded at the immense supplies of food the Indians possessed. In his official account of the expedition De Nonville stated that the

French officers had the curiosity to estimate the whole quantity of ripe and green corn they had destroyed in the Seneca villages and fields, and they found the total amount 400,000 minots or 1,200,000 bushels. This was undoubtedly an exaggerated statement, yet it illustrated the fruitful returns of native industry, and the prosperous condition of those Indians who depended upon agriculture for their main support.

Ninety-two years later, during the revolutionary war, General Sullivan led an army of 4000 men to the Genesee river to chastise the Senecas for their destructive raids upon the border settlements of New York and Pennsylvania. The principal town of the western Senecas, then known as the "Genesee castle," was located upon the present site of Cuylerville, and consisted of 128 houses. On the rich soil of the valley near at hand the Senecas had 200 acres of grain, large crops of beans, potatoes and other vegetables, and several orchards, one of which contained 1,500 trees. The great Genesee valley was an ideal Indian paradise where all their simple wants were fully supplied ; but Sullivan's soldiers destroyed everything of a nutritive nature, and at their departure did not leave in the locality food sufficient to save a child from starvation.

The deplorable circumstances of the Senecas, subsequent to these destructive invasions of the whites were fair examples of a condition to which these warlike people were constantly subject from enraged enemies. From riches and abundance they were liable at any moment to be reduced to poverty and starvation. In such emergencies their first recourse for food was wild game ; and during the season of scarcity their rude implements of husbandry were often employed to delve in uncultivated plains and unfrequented nooks of the forest, for esculent roots upon which they subsisted for long periods.

We learn something of the domestic habits of the Iroquois from the narration of Luke Swetland, who was a prisoner among the Senecas at Kendaia, near Seneca Lake, from August 1778, to September 1779, and who, after his release, published an account of his adventures. Regarding their means of subsistence Mr. Swetland says : "The Indians live in some respects as one family, on corn, beans, squashes and potatoes while those last, some meat, sugar, milk and butter ; but in the summer chiefly on ground nuts and other weeds and roots. Their country contains many lakes affording plenty of fish, salt sprin s where I made salt, a sort of root with which they make bread, they call it ook-te-haw, a great plenty of wild mandrakes, etc." [1]

1 Narrative of the captivity of Luke Swetland, among the Seneca Indians. 18.

Mr. Swetland gave little attention to the logical construction of sentences, and his statement "a sort of root from which they made bread, they call it ook-te-haw," leaves the reader—unversed in the Indian language—in doubt whether the term ook-te-haw applies to root or bread. In the Seneca dialect root is pronounced oke-tah'-a. Beets, carrots, parsnips, and turnips are all called roots and distinguished by their color, as oke-tah-a, root ; oke-tah-dane-yo, roots ; quin-tah-a, red ; jit-quâ-a, yellow ; no-wunt-dá-a, white. In some cases the name of a root is circumstantial, and either describes the particular root or explains its quality and use. The Seneca word for bread is o-ak'-qua. It would thus appear that the term ook-te-haw, if the orthography is correct, did not apply to either word, root or bread, in its specific sense. According to the Seneca principle[2] of uniting nouns and adjectives to form new words, the compound term for bread-root would be oke-tah-ak'-qua ; and it is clear that ook-te-haw was the proper name of a particular root then in such common use that a special description was deemed unnecessary ; our inquiry therefore, properly includes the identity of this root.

In writing of the root ook-te-haw Mr. Swetland evidently had no reference to either the potato (*Solanum tuberosum*) or the ground nut (*Apios tuberosa*) as he in several instances distinctly mentions those articles of food by their common names ; yet a partial history of these native plants is essential in our line of evidence.

Seneca tradition asserts that the Iroquois originally consisted of two tribes named after the bear and deer, each tribe using a picture or crude drawing of its appellative animal as a totem or clan mark. These tribes or clans increased in number and in the distribution of sachemships at the institution of the League, about the middle of the 15th century, eight distinct clans were recognized. The Paris Documents of 1666 contain an extended account of the Iroquois cantons at that date, and name nine tribes giving the title of the sixth as Scone-scheoronon or Potato people; the clan totem consisting of a string of potatoes. It is probable that this tribe was originally composed of captives whose special food consisted of potatoes, or whose particular business was the cultivation of that class of roots. Later designators of tribal names omit that of the Potato people, who had either received a new clan title, or been absorbed by other tribes.

An early historical mention of the potato is found in the journal of Thomas Herriot, who came to America in 1584 in the expedition of Sir Walter Raleigh. "Openawk," says Herriot, "are a kind of roots of round form, some of the bigness of walnuts, some far greater, which

---

2 Drop all letters following the initial consonant of the last syllable of the noun, and all letters following the first consonant of the adjective, then suffix the latter to the former.

are found in moist and marsh grounds, growing many together one by
another in ropes, as though they were fastened with a string. Being
boiled or sodden they are very good meat." The openawk was carried
to England on the return voyage in 1586, and in 1597 Gerard figured
the tuber in his Herbal under the name Potato of Virginia. From the
date of their first settlement in America the colonists propagated the
potato as a staple food, and at the middle of the 18th century it was
considered a product of agriculture by the whites, who regarded the
ground nut as a native or wild root. Contemporary tribes of red men
also recognized the distinction between the potato and ground nut
and gave a specific title to each plant. At the period of the revolutionary war the potato was cultivated by the Senecas who termed the
tuber o-nun-un-da and planted it with their corn, beans and squashes.
The modern Seneca term is o-no-nok'-dah ; and many of the present
generation of Indians regard the potato and ground nut as one species
and apply the same name to both.

In his Travels in North America, in 1749, Professor Kalm writes :
"at the first arrival of the Swedes in this country, and long after, it
was filled with Indians. * * The food of these Indians was very
different from that of the inhabitants of other parts of the world.
Wheat, rye, barley, oats, and rice groats, were quite unknown in
America. * * The maize, some kinds of beans and melons, made
almost the whole of the Indian agriculture. * * Hop-nis was the
Indian name of a wild plant which they ate at that time. The Swedes
now call it by that name and it still grows in the meadows. The roots
resemble potatoes. They were boiled by the Indians, who ate them
instead of bread. Some of the Swedes likewise ate them for want of
bread. Some of the English still eat them instead of potatoes. * *
Dr. Linneas calls the plant *Glycine apious*."

The narrative of the Gilbert Family captured in Pennsylvania and
brought through the Genesee region in 1780, describes the arrival of
the party in the vicinity of Canandaigua where " necessity induced two
of the Indians to set off on horseback, into the Seneca country, in
search of provisions. The prisoners, in the meantime, were ordered to
dig up a root, something resembling potatoes, which the Indians called
whop-pan-ies. They tarried at this place until towards evening of the
succeeding day and made a soup of wild onions and turnip tops ; this
they eat without bread or salt. * * They left this place and crossed
the Genesee river * * They fixed their station near the Genesee
banks and procured more of the wild potato roots before mentioned
for their supper."

The name hop-nis, as rendered by Professor Kalm who obtained it from Indians on the Susquehanna river, and the term whop-pan-ies as used in the Gilbert narrative, differ in orthography, but the pronunciation of the two words is so nearly alike there can be no reasonable doubt of their identity. The modern Seneca for ground nut is yo-a-jah-go-o, which is interpreted, "being always in the ground."

An extended study of the subject impresses the writer with a belief that the bread root mentioned by Luke Swetland, can be identified as *Arum*[1] *triphyllum* of the botanist, commonly known as Indian

FLOWER AND FRUIT OF ARUM TRIPHYLLUM, AND O-A-O-SAH OR BABY-BOARD.

turnip, and variously termed three-leaved arum, wake robin, dragon root, pepper turnip, swamp turnip, starchworth, bog onion, priest's pintle, lord and ladies, jack in the pulpit, etc. This plant possesses every essential of nativity and quality requisite for a bread root, such as may have been used by the Indians during Swetland's enforced residence among them. It grows in damp woods, in swamps, in low

1. The name Arisæma is said to be a play upon the older name Arum. Torrey's Flora.

meadows, along ditches and in moist, shady places. It is well known to all lovers of wild plants as a floral curio, both on account of its peculiar flower and acrimonious nature. The root is roundish, flattened, an inch or two in diameter, covered with a brown, loose, wrinkled epidermis, and internally white, fleshy and solid. In its fresh state it is violently acrid, producing, when chewed, an insupportable burning and biting sensation in the mouth and throat, which continues for a long time, leaving an unpleasant soreness. It is used when fresh, and may be preserved a year by packing in damp sand. When dried and pulverized it produces a beautiful snow white powder, that when properly prepared, may be employed as a substitute for flour in making bread.

For many years the Senecas have called this plant "baby board," from its resemblance in form to the board used by Indian mothers as a convenience in the transportation of infants. The frame of a baby board is about two feet long, fourteen to sixteen inches wide, has a narrow shelf or foot-rest at the lower end and a hoop arched at right angles over the head. The infant is wrapped in a blanket and lashed to the board with broad belts. A small cloth is then drawn over the upper end and hoop, forming a hood that leaves the face of the child exposed yet secure from the weather. This board is termed o-a-o-sah. The peculiar shape of Arum triphyllum always attracts the attention of Indians who hold up their hands and say : " Just like baby board, that flower !" [1] hence they apply the name o-a-o-sah to the visible portion of the plant, but the part below the surface of the ground is known simply as oke-tah´-a, a root. It is probable that Swetland mis-pronounced the smooth flowing Seneca word o-a-o-sah, rendering it, in crude Yankee vernacular, ook-te-haw.

At the period of which Mr. Swetland wrote, the Senecas were associated with the British, in their efforts to subdue the American colonists, and received some aid from their English allies ; but as a people they were mainly uncultivated nomads of the forest, characterized by the same habits and customs their ancestors had possessed for unknown centuries, dependent upon their skill as hunters and, to some extent, upon the natural productions of the soil. Our inquiry regarding the identity of ook-te-haw may, therefore, extend to the customs and diet of their forefathers as recorded in early chronicles.

In Thomas Herriot's account of Virginia in 1585, that writer informs us that "Cos-cus-haw * * groweth in very muddy pools and moist grounds. * * The juice is poison, and therefore heed must be taken before anything be made therewithal ; either the roots must be first sliced

---

1 The writer gratefully acknowledges his obligations to J. H. Van Valkenburg, Superintendent of the Thomas Asylum at Cattaraugus, to Solomon O'Bail, A. Sim Logan and William P. Buck for interpretations of various Seneca terms.

and dried. and then being pounded into flour, will make good bread ; or else while they are green they are to be pared, cut in pieces and stamped : loaves of the same to be laid near or over the fire until sour, and then being well pounded again, bread or spoon-meat, very good in taste and very wholesome, may be made thereof."

Captain John Smith's Virginia, 1606, says :—" The chief root they (the Indians) have for food is called loc-ka-whough. It grows in the marshes * * and is much of the greatness and taste of potatoes. * * Raw, it is no better than poison, and being roasted. except it be tender and the heat abated, mixed with sorrel or meal, it will prick and torment the throat extremely ; yet in summer they use this ordinarily for bread." Carver's Travels in North America, 1766, says : " Wake Robin is an herb that grows in swampy lands, its root resembles a small turnip and, if tasted, will greatly inflame the tongue, and immediately convert it from its natural shape into a round hard substance ; but when dried it looses its astringent quality and becomes beneficial to mankind."

" Taw-ho and taw-him." wrote Kalm. " is the Indian name of a plant the root of which they eat. * * Some call it tuc-kah. The roots are reckoned poison in a fresh state, * * but when prepared (by roasting) taste like potatoes. * * This taw-ho is the *Arum Virginicum*, or Virginian wake-robin, and seems to be the same plant the Indians in Carolina call tuc-ka-hoo. * * A stranger from Carolina gave Mr. John Bartram the following description of tuc-ka-hoo :—' It grows in swamps, marshes and woods, and the Indians in Carolina, in their rambles, gather the roots, dry them in the sunshine, grind and bake bread of them. While the root is fresh it is harsh and acrid, but being dried it loses its acrimony.' To judge by these qualities the tuc-ka-hoo may very likely be the *Arum Virginicum*. * * The Indians are very fond of turnips and call them sometimes hop-nis, sometimes kat-nis. * * Throughout the summer before the Swedes came. their hopnis or the roots of *Glycine apious*, their katnis or roots of *Sagittaria sagittifolia*, their tawho or roots of *Arum Virginicum*, their tawkee or *Orontium aquaticum*, and whortleberries, were their chief food."

The above accounts of the old writers are conclusive, that the aboriginal inhabitants of Virginia and Pennsylvania used *Arum Virginicum* as a material for bread. The variation of *A. Virginicum* and *A. triphyllum*, is so trifling that some authorities class them as one. The great aboriginal water communication between Lake Ontario and the Atlantic was through the Seneca country to the Susquehanna river ;

thence, via Chesapeake bay to the Ocean, and it is well understood that the Indians of New York, Pennsylvania and Virginia were in constant intercourse (in fact the Iroquois claimed the country from Lake Ontario south to the Tennessee river), and that the customs and foods of the natives of those sections were in many respects the same. Swetland, unfortunately, gives no description of the root he calls ook-te-haw ; but evidence in the hands of the writer shows that the pioneers of the Genesee Valley and County of Ontario, used the Indian turnip *Arum triphyllum* as a substitute for flour, and that they obtained their knowledge of the manner of preparing this root from Seneca Indians. It would seem that the cos-cus-haw of Herriot, the loc-ka-whough of Smith, the wake-robin of Carver, the tuc-ka-hoo of the South, the taw-ho of Kalm, the o-a-o-sah of the Senecas and the ook-te-haw of Swetland, were identical and that the bread root mentioned by Luke Swetland was *Arum triphyllum.*

Was it not a pressing necessity, that first induced aboriginal man to test the nutritious qualities of the most nauseous of all wild plants *Symplocarpus fœtidus,* commonly known as pole-cat root or skunk cabbage ? The early Swedish settlers on the Susquehanna river called this plant, byron blad, or bear's leaf, and some termed it byron retter, or bear's root, from the fact that bears on leaving their winter habitations in the spring were excessively fond of it. The early Senecas called the plant o-sha-ta. They used the root for all purposes of food and medicine where arum could be employed. As a bread root it was roasted or baked to extract the juice, in much the same manner as arum. When the Seneca towns were destroyed by General Sullivan in 1779, the Indians found themselves utterly destitute and many moved to Fort Niagara where the British fed them, mainly on salt meats, during the following winter. As a result hundreds died of scurvy ; but those who used the root of skunk cabbage as an anti-scorbutic, recovered their health.

That beautiful and curious plant, Solomon's seal, was also a welcome addition to the aboriginal larder in times of necessity. Many years ago a Seneca who was roving over the ground now named Highland Park, in this city, called the attention of his boy companion, the late John Nutt, to Solomon's seal as a plant once highly prized by Indians. He said it was formerly much used by the Senecas as a medicine, and that they also boiled the young shoots in the spring and ate them. The mature roots were gathered in the fall, dried, ground or pounded, and made into bread.

The method of manufacturing bread from roots was very simple. After the roots had been thoroughly dried and pulverized the flour was seasoned, mixed with a little animal or fish fat, moistened, worked into a pastry dough and patted into the form of a cake or loaf, which was placed on a piece of bark or flat stone turned up on its side close to the fire. Occasionally the stone was heated and the cake was thus at once baked on both sides. Sometimes the loaf was baked in a kettle or placed in the ashes under a cover of hot coals : and the individual who objected to eating the mass as it came from the fire with its covering of gritty ashes, was considered a person of poor taste and quite ill bred.

There is a question regarding the identification of an Indian bread root that is worthy the attention of the botanical section of this Academy. In narrating the privations suffered by the whites who settled on the Chenango river in 1788, Wilkinson's Annals of Binghampton says, that when their crops of corn failed and festive bruin had devastated their pig styes, the starving settlers went to an island in the river, and dug quantities of a tall weed termed Anicum, the roots of which they dried and ground or pounded into a coarse flour for bread-stuff.

It is possible that this so-called anicum was a species of the genus *Panicum* or panic grass, the seeds of which the wild Indians of the West still use for bread in the same manner white people use wheat : but the writer cannot learn that the seeds of anacum were utilized for food. Inquiries resulted in the description of a plant in many respects resembling *Psoralea esculenta*, commonly known in the western States as Indian bread root, prairie turnip, etc. Botanical authorities usually report *Psoralea esculenta* a native of the West and South ; but a Seneca friend who had visited the Sioux Indians and was familiar with their bread root tip-si-u-nah, which plant possesses none of the poisonous qualities of arum, positively assured the writer that such a plant once grew in New York. A public agitation of the bread root topic last summer, was productive of the following letter from General J. S. Clark, the distinguished Indianologist and botanist, to Hon. George S. Conover of Geneva :

AUBURN, N. Y., July 11, 1890.

Dear Sir :—You are at liberty to state that *Psoralea esculenta* has been found in New York, in Washington county, many years ago by Mr. Frank R. Rathbun, of this city, and fully identified as the genuine plant growing in its wild state. A little more inquiry will probably establish the fact, that it has been discovered in other localities and may now be found in Central New York. I fully believe, however, that Luke Swetland's ook-te-haw is the well-known Indian turnip.

Very respectfully,   JOHN S. CLARK.

In response to a request for particulars General Clark forwarded a letter from Mr. Rathbun from which we extract the following :— "The plant in question was found by myself, in the early summer of 1856 or 1857, at Fort Edward, Washington Co., N. Y., west of the Collegiate Institute, in a moist situation near the location, of the Jane McRea spring. As something unique, I carried the bulb, flower or seed vessel and leaves, to the Professor of Natural History at the Institute for analysis, before the class in botany. Pronounced by him a rare find, something new. I recollect he seemed surprised ; also recollect the specific term *esculenta* or Indian bread root applied to the specimen. His name was Solomon Sias. By the last Naturalists' Directory I find his address to be Schoharie, N. Y., (Solomon Sias, A. M., M. D.)"

It is well known that the flora of New York, has changed greatly during the past hundred years, and it may be an interesting question for our botanical section to decide, whether *Psoralea esculenta* can be added to the list of extinct plants.

The yellow pond lily, now so greatly admired as an aquatic flower, is a native of marshes, and the Senecas who frequented Irondequoit bay often procured the roots from the marsh-beds that surrounded that beautiful and historic sheet of water. The roots are large, sweet, and glutinous and not an unpleasant food when boiled or roasted and eaten with wild fowl or meat ; or if well seasoned with salt. The lily was known to the early Senecas as o-was-oos-hah, a word almost identical in sound with the native name (o-a-o-sah) of arum or baby board ; but the writer has been unable to learn the meaning of the term as applied to this particular flower.

Musk rats, which once abounded in all the shallow waters of the Genesee country, stored quantities of the lily roots in their rude houses for winter support ; and it was the usual custom of the Indians when hunting the little water animals, to search their houses for the roots. It is a fact, well attested by men who have been familiarly associated with Indians and accustomed to their food, that when properly dressed to remove the rank odor, the flesh of the musk rat is excellent meat ; and the Senecas doubtless had good reasons for heartily enjoying their winter dishes of ju-no-dá-gá, or musk rat flesh, and o-was-oos-hah, or pond lily root.

A more extended list of root foods might be presented, but a sufficient number has already been described. The hungry aborigines

satisfied the cravings of appetite with all manner of vegetation not
absolutely poisonous, and rendered edible many plants and roots of a
known poisonous nature, by maceration in cold and hot water, and by
baking and frying ; thus evaporating the deadly juices and nullifying the
unpalatable characteristics. Vegetable matter reduced by such means is
usually insipid, and the Indians often resorted to various expedients for
seasoning. Salt was the principal and natural recourse. There were sev-
several saline springs in the territory of the Sencas besides those east of
Seneca lake mentioned by Luke Swetland. The Indians of the Genesee
Valley often came to Irondequoit bay to make salt. There was a salt
spring at the head of the bay on the west side, one in Dunbar hollow, and
others east of the bay. The last one used by the Senecas was located
in Webster, south of Forest Lawn. When the Senecas retired to reservations about 1796, an old chief from Moscow, in company with Jacob
Walker the tory first-resident of Irondequoit, covered the Webster
spring with stone, so effectually concealing it that it remains undiscovered to this day.

As substitutes for salt the Indians used the white portion of hard
wood ashes, the ashes of corn cobs and certain leaves, and occasionally
the lye of wood ashes. Fish, animal fat, and oils produced from nuts
were also employed to modify the unpleasant qualities of root foods.
The meats of nuts were often mashed into a sort of butter-grease
for seasoning. Butternuts especially were reduced to a thin milk that
was considered nourishing for infants and children. Other vegetable
matter, such as acorns and dandelion roots, was roasted, pounded and
sprinkled over the cooked roots. Squash rinds, corn meal and maple
sugar were dainties. Horse-radish was boiled with meats as well as
roots, and mints and cress proved acceptable relishes.

Acids were supplied by wild fruits and berries when those could
be obtained. A loaf of root bread well sprinkled with berries was not
to be sneezed at. The sumach also provided an agreeable wholesome
acid. It was called ote-kó-dá, by the Senecas who were careful to select
the red-berried sumach, as the white-berried species is poisonous It
was a happy day when the hungry root-eater discovered a nest of black
ants. The insects were called je-hus-to-qua The Indians laid upon
the nests pieces of freshly peeled bark upon which the ants gathered in
large numbers and were at once secured. The sharp vinegar like taste
of the insects was a great incentive to appetite.

The kâ-no was, or cow-slip, the o-nah-sâ, or mushroon, the o-nus-
tá-sah, or sassafras, the green shoots of o-nó-to-wâ-nes, or the burdock,
the ya-ho, or mandrake, the jes-tâ-ga-â-go-wâ, or wintergreen, the

beech, willow, basswood and gooseberry, the ground
-sâ, or the sunflower, were all utilized as relishes,
ases, as substitutes for solid foods.

various nations of Indians that now roam the plains
the West, with the unrestrained freedom of ancient
he old time habits and customs still prevail, and whole
tu.⸻, a precarious existence upon vegetable diets consisting
mainly of c⸻ulent roots ; but the reservation Indians of the State of
New York have long been dependent for subsistance upon the products
of intelligent agriculture, and even the legendary knowledge of ances-
tral foods has in many instances utterly faded from remembrance.
Occasionally an educated Indian will cast a gleam of light upon the
dark kitchen mysteries of his progenitors, and now and then the
student of aboriginal history discovers a diamond of knowledge in the
crooning of some aged Seneca who cherishes a memory of the strange
habits and stranger tastes of his wild-wood forefathers.